Classics

JOHN COOPER.

THE CORAL ISLAND

THE CORAL ISLAND

A Tale of the Pacific Ocean

R. M. Ballantyne

Published by Priory Books, Bridlington.
A Peter Haddock Limited imprint.
© Blackie & Son Ltd.
Printed in Hungary

In this edition of the classic *The Coral Island* some of the author's reflections have been curtailed or omitted, and the episodes after the three heroes get away from the island have been dropped, as being in the nature of an anticlimax; the book, as a story, is improved by their omission.

CHAPTER I

Roving has always been, and still is, my ruling passion, the joy of my heart, the very sunshine of my existence. In childhood, in boyhood, and in man's estate, I have been a rover; not a mere rambler among the woody glens and upon the hilltops of my own native land, but an enthusiastic rover throughout the length and breadth of the wide, wide world.

Soon after I was born, my father, being old, retired from a seafaring life, purchased a small cottage in a fishing village on the west coast of England, and settled down to spend the evening of his life on the shores of that sea which had for so many years been his home. It was not long before I began to show the roving spirit that dwelt within me, until at last I had wandered far and near on the shore and in the woods around our humble dwelling, and did not rest content until my father bound me apprentice to a coasting vessel, and let me go to sea.

For some years I was happy in visiting the sea-ports, and in coasting along the shores of my native land. My Christian name was Ralph, and my comrades added to this the name of Rover. They were kind, good-natured fellows, and they and I got on very well together.

Now, while engaged in the coasting trade, I fell in with many seamen who had travelled to almost every quarter of the globe; and my heart glowed ardently within me as they recounted their wild adventures in foreign lands—the dreadful storms they had weathered, the appalling dangers they had escaped, the wonderful creatures they had seen both on the land and in the sea, and the interesting lands and strange people they had visited. But of all the places of which they told me, none captivated and charmed my imagination so much as the Coral Islands of the Southern Seas. They told me of thousands of beautiful fertile islands that had been formed by a small creature called the coral insect, where summer reigned nearly all the year round; where the trees were laden with a constant harvest of luxuriant fruit; where the climate was almost perpetually delightful; yet where, strange to say, men were wild, bloodthirsty savages, excepting in those favoured isles to which the gospel of our Saviour had been conveyed. These exciting accounts had so great an effect upon my mind, that, when I reached the age of fifteen, I resolved to make a voyage to the South Seas.

I had no little difficulty at first in prevailing on my dear parents to let me go; but when I urged on my father that he would never have become a great captain had he remained in the coasting trade, he saw the truth of what I said, and gave his consent. My dear mother, seeing that my father had made up his mind, no longer offered opposition to my wishes. 'But oh, Ralph,' she said, on the day I bade her adieu, 'come back soon to us, my dear boy, for we are getting old now, Ralph, and may not have many years to live.'

Soon afterwards I went on board the *Arrow*, which was a fine large ship, and set sail for the islands of the Pacific Ocean.

CHAPTER II

It was a bright, beautiful, warm day when our ship spread her canvas to the breeze, and sailed for the regions of the south.

The first thing that struck me as being different from anything I had yet seen during my short career on the sea, was the hoisting of the anchor on deck, and lashing it firmly down with ropes, as if we had now bid adieu to the land for ever, and would require its services no more.

'There, lass,' cried a broad-shouldered jack-tar, giving the fluke of the anchor a hearty slap with his hand after the housing was completed—'there, lass, take a good nap now, for we shan't ask you to kiss the mud again for many a long day to come!'

There were a number of boys in the ship, but two of them

were my special favourites. Jack Martin was a tall, strapping, broad-shouldered youth of eighteen, with a handsome, good-humoured, firm face. He had had a good education, was clever and hearty and lion-like in his actions, but mild and quiet in disposition. Jack was a general favourite, and had a peculiar fondness for me. My other companion was Peterkin Gay. He was little, quick, funny, decidedly mischievous, and about fourteen years old. But Peterkin's mischief was almost always harmless, else he could not have been so much beloved as he was.

'Hallo, youngster!' cried Jack Martin, giving me a slap on the shoulder, the day I joined the ship, 'come below, and I'll show you your berth. You and I are to be messmates, and I think we shall be good friends, for I like the look o' you.'

Jack was right. He and I and Peterkin afterwards became the best and stanchest friends that ever tossed together on the stormy waves.

When we approached Cape Horn, at the southern extremity of America, the weather became very cold and stormy, and the sailors began to tell stories about the furious gales and the dangers of that terrible cape.

Nevertheless, we passed the dreaded cape without much rough weather, and, in the course of a few weeks afterwards, were sailing gently before a warm tropical breeze over the Pacific Ocean. Thus we proceeded on our voyage, sometimes bounding merrily before a fair breeze, at other times floating calmly on the glassy wave and fishing for the curious inhabitants of the deep—all of which, although the sailors thought little of them, were strange, and interesting, and very wonderful to me.

At last we came among the Coral Islands of the Pacific, and I shall never forget the delight with which I gazed—when we chanced to pass one—at the pure, white, dazzling shores, and the verdant palm trees, which looked bright and beautiful in the sunshine. And often did we three long to be landed on one, imagining that we should certainly find perfect happiness there! Our wish was granted sooner than we expected.

One night, soon after we entered the tropics, an awful storm burst upon our ship. The first squall of wind carried away two of our masts, and left only the foremast standing. Even this, however, was more than enough, for we did not dare to hoist a rag of sail on it. For five days the tempest raged in all its fury. Everything was swept off the decks except one small boat. The steersman was lashed to the wheel, lest he should be washed away, and we all gave ourselves up for lost. The captain said that he had no idea where we were, as we had been blown far out of our course; and we feared much that we might get among the dangerous coral reefs which are so numerous in the Pacific. At daybreak on the sixth morning of the gale we saw land ahead. It was an island encircled by a reef of coral on which the waves broke in fury. There was calm water within this reef, but we could only see one narrow opening into it. For this opening we steered, but ere we reached it a tremendous wave broke on our stern, tore the rudder completely off, and left us at the mercy of the winds and waves.

'It's all over with us now, lads!' said the captain to the men. 'Get the boat ready to launch; we shall be on the rocks in less than half an hour.'

The men obeyed in gloomy silence, for they felt that there was little hope of so small a boat living in such a sea.

'Come, boys,' said Jack Martin, in a grave tone, to me and Peterkin, as we stood on the quarter-deck awaiting our fate—'come, boys; we three shall stick together. You see it is impossible that the little boat can reach the shore, crowded with men. It will be sure to upset, so I mean rather to trust myself to a large oar. I see through the telescope that the ship will strike at the tail of the reef, where the waves break into the quiet water inside; so, if we manage to cling to the oar till it is driven over the breakers, we may perhaps gain the shore. What say you; will you join me?'

We gladly agreed to follow Jack, for he inspired us with confidence, although I could perceive, by the sad tone of his voice, that he had little hope; and indeed, when I looked at the white waves that lashed the reef and boiled against the rocks as if in fury, I felt that there was but a step between us and death.

The ship was now very near the rocks. The men were ready with the boat, and the captain beside them giving orders, when a tremendous wave came towards us. We three ran towards the bow to lay hold of our oar, and had barely reached it when the wave fell on the deck with a crash like thunder. At the same moment the ship struck, the foremast broke off close to the deck and went over the side, carrying the boat and men along with it. Our oar got entangled with the wreck, and Jack seized an axe to cut it free, but, owing to the motion of the ship, he missed the cordage and struck the axe deep into the oar. Another wave, however, washed it clear of the wreck. We all seized hold of it, and the next instant we were struggling in the wild sea. The last thing I saw was the boat whirling in the surf, and all the sailors tossed into the foaming waves. Then I became insensible.

On recovering from my swoon, I found myself lying on a bank of soft grass, under the shelter of an overhanging rock, with Peterkin on his knees by my side, tenderly bathing my temples with water, and endeavouring to stop the blood that flowed from a wound in my forehead.

CHAPTER III

As I slowly recovered and heard the voice of Peterkin in-quiring whether I felt better, I thought that I must have over-slept myself, and should be sent to the masthead for being lazy; but before I could leap up in haste, the thought seemed to vanish suddenly away, and I fancied that I must have been ill.

I now raised myself on my elbow, and putting my hand to my forehead, found that it had been cut pretty severely, and that I had lost a good deal of blood.

'Come, come, Ralph,' said Jack, pressing me gently back-ward, 'lie down, my boy. Wet your lips with this water; it's cool and clear as crystal. I got it from a spring close at hand. There now, don't say a word, hold your tongue,' said he, seeing me about to speak. 'I'll tell you all about it, but you must not utter a syllable till you have rested well.'

'Let him speak, Jack.' said Peterkin; 'it's a comfort to hear that he's alive, after lying there stiff and white and sulky for a whole hour, just like an Egyptian mummy. Never saw such a fellow as you are, Ralph; always up to mischief. You've almost knocked out all my teeth and more than half choked me, and now you go shamming death. It's very wicked of you, indeed it is.'

While Peterkin ran on in this style, my faculties became quite clear again, and I began to understand my position. 'What do you mean by saying I half choked you, Peterkin?' said I.

'What do I mean? Is English not your mother-tongue, or do you want me to repeat it in French, by way of making it clearer? Don't you remember——'

'I remember nothing,' said I, interrupting him, 'after we were thrown into the sea.'

'Hush, Peterkin,' said Jack 'you're exciting Ralph with your nonsense.—I'll explain it to you. You recollect that after the ship struck, we three sprang over the bow into the sea: well, I noticed that the oar struck your head and gave you that cut on the brow, which nearly stunned you, so that you grasped Peterkin round the neck without knowing apparently what you were about. In doing so you pushed the telescope—which you clung to as if it had been your life—against Peterkin's mouth——'

'Pushed it against his mouth!' interrupted Peterkin; 'say crammed it down his throat. Why, there's a distinct mark of the brass rim on the back of my gullet at this moment!'

'Well, well, be that as it may,' continued Jack, 'you clung to him, Ralph, till I feared you really would choke him; but I saw that he had a good hold of the oar, so I tried my utmost to push you towards the shore, which we luckily reached without much trouble, for the water inside the reef is quite calm.'

'But the captain and crew, what of them?' I inquired anxiously.

Jack shook his head.

'Are they lost?'

'I fear there is not much chance of their being saved. The ship struck at the very tail of the island on which we are cast. When the boat was tossed into the sea it fortunately did not upset, although it shipped a good deal of water, and all the men managed to scramble into it; but before they could get

the oars out the gale carried them past the point and away
to leeward of the island. After we landed I saw them endeavouring to pull towards us; but as they had only one pair of oars
out of the eight that belong to the boat, and as the wind was
blowing right in their teeth, they gradually lost ground. Then
I saw them put about and hoist some sort of sail—a blanket,
I fancy, for it was too small for the boat—and in half an hour
they were out of sight.'

'Poor fellows!' I murmured sorrowfully.

'But the more I think about it, I've better hope of them,'
continued Jack, in a more cheerful tone. 'You see, Ralph,
I've read a great deal about these South Sea Islands, and I
know that in many places they are scattered about in thousands
over the sea, so they're almost sure to fall in with one of them
before long.'

'I'm sure I hope so,' said Peterkin earnestly. 'But what
has become of the wreck, Jack? I saw you clambering up the
rocks there while I was watching Ralph. Did you say she had
gone to pieces?'

'No, she has not gone to pieces, but she has gone to the
bottom,' replied Jack. 'She struck on the tail of the island and
stove in her bow, but the next breaker swung her clear, and
she floated away to leeward and foundered.'

There was a long silence after Jack ceased speaking, and
I have no doubt that each was revolving in his mind our extraordinary position. For my part, I cannot say that my reflections were very agreeable. I knew that we were on an island,
for Jack had said so, but whether it was inhabited or not I did
not know. If it should be inhabited, I felt certain, from all I
had heard of South Sea Islanders, that we should be roasted
alive and eaten. If it should turn out to be uninhabited, I
fancied that we should be starved to death.

'Well,' said Jack, 'we are certainly in rather an uncomfortable position. If this is a desert island, we shall have to
live very much like the wild beasts, for we have not a tool of
any kind, not even a knife.'

'Yes, we have *that*,' said Peterkin, fumbling in his trousers
pocket, from which he drew forth a small penknife with only
one blade, and that was broken.

'Well, that's better than nothing. But come,' said Jack, rising; 'we are wasting our time in *talking* instead of *doing*.— You seem well enough to walk now, Ralph.—Let us see what we have got in our pockets, and then let us climb some hill and ascertain what sort of island we have been cast upon, for, whether good or bad, it seems likely to be our home for some time to come.'

CHAPTER IV

We now seated ourselves upon a rock, and began to examine into our personal property. When we reached the shore, after being wrecked, my companions had taken off part of their clothes and spread them out in the sun to dry; for although the gale was raging fiercely, there was not a single cloud in the bright sky. They had also stripped off most part of my wet clothes and spread them also on the rocks. Having resumed our garments, we now searched all our pockets with the utmost care, and laid their contents out on a flat stone before us; and now that our minds were fully alive to our condition, it was with no little anxiety that we turned our several pockets inside out, in order that nothing might escape us. When all was collected together, we found that our worldly goods consisted of the following articles:—

First, A small penknife with a single blade broken off about the middle and very rusty, besides having two or three notches on its edge. (Peterkin said of this, with his usual pleasantry, that it would do for a saw as well as a knife, which was a great advantage.) Second, An old German-silver pencil-case without any lead in it. Third, A piece of whip-cord about six yards long. Fourth, A sailmaker's needle of a small size. Fifth, A ship's telescope, which I happened to have in my hand at the time the ship struck, and which I had clung to firmly all the time I was in the water. Indeed, it was with difficulty that Jack got it out of my grasp when I was lying insensible on the shore. We felt some pleasure in having it, although we did not see that it could be of much use to us, as the glass at the small end was broken to pieces. Our sixth article was a brass ring which Jack always wore on his little finger. In addition to these articles we had a little bit of tinder, and the clothes on our backs. This was all we had. When we thought of the danger we had escaped, and how much worse off we might have been had the ship struck the reef during the night, we felt thankful that we possessed so much.

While we were examining these things and talking about them, Jack suddenly started and exclaimed:

'The oar! we have forgotten the oar.'

'What good will that do us?' said Peterkin; 'there's wood enough on the island to make a thousand oars.'

'Ay, lad,' replied Jack; 'but there's a bit of hoop iron at the end of it, and that may be of much use to us.'

'Very true,' said I, 'let us go fetch it;' and with that we all three rose and hastened down to the beach. I still felt a little weak from loss of blood, so that my companions soon began to leave me behind; but Jack perceived this, and, with his usual good nature, turned back to help me. This was now the first time that I had looked well about me since landing, as the spot where I had been laid was covered with thick bushes, which almost hid the country from our view. As we now emerged from among these and walked down the sandy beach together, I cast my eyes about, and truly my heart glowed within me and my spirits rose at the beautiful prospect which I beheld on every side. The gale had suddenly died away, just as if it had blown furiously till it dashed our ship upon the rocks, and had nothing more to do after accomplishing that. The island on which we stood was hilly, and covered almost everywhere with the most beautiful and richly coloured trees, bushes, and shrubs, none of which I knew the names of at that time, except, indeed, the cocoa-nut palms, which I recognized at once from the many pictures that I had seen of them before I left home. A sandy beach of dazzling whiteness lined this bright green shore, and upon it there fell a gentle ripple of the sea. This last astonished me much, for I recollected that at home the sea used to fall in huge billows on the shore long after a storm had subsided. But on casting my glance out to sea the cause became apparent. About a mile distant from the shore I saw the great billows of the ocean rolling like a green wall, and falling with a long, loud roar upon a low coral reef, where they were dashed into white foam and flung up in clouds of spray. This spray sometimes flew exceedingly high, and every here and there a beautiful rainbow was formed for a moment among the falling drops. We afterwards found that this coral reef extended quite round the island, and formed a natural breakwater to it. Beyond this the sea rose and tossed violently from the effects of the storm; but between the reef and the shore it was as calm and as smooth as a pond.

While we gazed at the scene, we were startled by a loud 'Huzza!' from Peterkin, and on looking towards the edge of the sea, we saw him capering and jumping about like a monkey, and ever and anon tugging with all his might at something that lay upon the shore.

'What an odd fellow he is, to be sure!' said Jack, taking me by the arm and hurrying forward; 'come, let us hasten to see what it is.'

'Here it is, boys, hurrah! come along. Just what we want,' cried Peterkin, as we drew near, still tugging with all his power. 'First rate; just the very ticket!'

On coming up we found that Peterkin was vainly endeavouring to pull the axe out of the oar, into which, it will be remembered, Jack struck it while endeavouring to cut away the cordage among which it had become entangled at the bow of the ship. Fortunately for us the axe had remained fast in the oar, and even now all Peterkin's strength could not draw it out of the cut.

'Ah! that is capital indeed,' cried Jack, at the same time giving the axe a wrench that plucked it out of the tough wood. 'How fortunate this is! It will be of more value to us than a hundred knives, and the edge is quite new and sharp.'

'I'll answer for the toughness of the handle at any rate,' cried Peterkin; 'my arms are nearly pulled out of the sockets. But see here, our luck is great. There is iron on the blade.' He pointed to a piece of hoop iron as he spoke, which had been nailed round the blade of the oar to prevent it from splitting.

This also was a fortunate discovery. Jack went down on his knees, and with the edge of the axe began carefully to force out the nails. But as they were firmly fixed in, and the operation blunted our axe, we carried the oar up with us to the place where we had left the rest of our things, intending to burn the wood away from the iron at a more convenient time.

'Now, lads,' said Jack, after we had laid it on the stone which contained our little all, 'I propose that we should go to the tail of the island, where the ship struck, which is only a quarter of a mile off, and see if anything else has been thrown ashore. I don't expect anything, but it is well to see. When we get back here it will be time to have our supper and prepare our beds.'

'Agreed!' cried Peterkin and I together.

Now, as we hastened along the white beach, which shone so brightly in the rays of the setting sun that our eyes were quite dazzled by its glare, it suddenly came into Peterkin's head that we had nothing to eat except the wild berries which grew in profusion at our feet.

'What shall we do, Jack?' said he, with a rueful look; 'perhaps they may be poisonous!'

'No fear,' replied Jack confidently; 'some of them are not unlike some of the berries that grow wild at home. Besides, I saw one or two strange birds eating them just a few minutes ago, and what won't kill the birds won't kill us. But look up there, Peterkin,' continued Jack, pointing to the branched head of a cocoa-nut palm. 'There are nuts for us in all stages.'

'So there are!' cried Peterkin, who, being of a very unobservant nature, had been too much taken up with other things to notice anything so high above his head as the fruit of a palm tree. But whatever faults my young comrade had, he could not be blamed for want of activity or animal spirits. Indeed, the nuts had scarcely been pointed out to him when he bounded up the tall stem of the tree like a squirrel, and in a few minutes returned with three nuts, each as large as a man's fist.

'You had better keep them till we return,' said Jack. 'Let us finish our work before eating.'

'So be it, captain; go ahead,' cried Peterkin, thrusting the nuts into his trousers pocket. 'In fact, I don't want to eat just now, but I would give a good deal for a drink. Oh that I could find a spring! but I don't see the smallest sign of one hereabouts. I say, Jack, how does it happen that you seem to be up to everything? You have told us the names of half a dozen trees already, and yet you say you were never in the South Seas before.'

'I'm not up to *everything*, Peterkin, as you'll find out ere long,' replied Jack, with a smile; 'but I have been a great reader of books of travel and adventure all my life, and that has put me up to a good many things that you are, perhaps, not acquainted with.'

'Oh, Jack, that's all humbug. If you begin to lay everything to the credit of books, I'll quite lose my opinion of you,' cried Peterkin, with a look of contempt. 'I've seen a lot of fellows that were always poring over books, and when they came to try to do anything, they were no better than baboons!'

'You are quite right,' retorted Jack; 'and I have seen a lot of fellows who never looked into books at all, who knew nothing about anything except the things they had actually seen, and very little they knew even about these. Indeed, some were so ignorant that they did not know that cocoa-nuts grew on cocoa-nut trees!'

'Humph! maybe you're right,' answered Peterkin; 'but I would not give tuppence for a man of books, if he had nothing else in him.'

'Neither would I,' said Jack; 'but that's no reason why you should run books down, or think less of me for having read them. Suppose, now, Peterkin, that you wanted to build a ship, and I were to give you a long and particular account of the way to do it, would not that be very useful?'

'No doubt of it,' said Peterkin, laughing.

'And suppose I were to write the account in a letter instead of telling you in words, would that be less useful?'

"Well—no, perhaps not.'

'Well, suppose I were to print it, and send it to you in the form of a book, would it not be as good and useful as ever?'

'Oh, bother! Jack, you're a philosopher, and that's worse

than anything!' cried Peterkin, with a look of pretended horror.

'Very well, Peterkin, we shall see,' returned Jack, halting under the shade of a cocoa-nut tree. 'You said you were thirsty just a minute ago; now jump up that tree and bring down a nut—not a ripe one, bring a green, unripe one.'

Peterkin looked surprised, but seeing that Jack was in earnest, he obeyed.

'Now cut a hole in it with your penknife, and clap it to your mouth, old fellow,' said Jack.

Peterkin did as he was directed, and no sooner had he put the nut to his mouth, and thrown back his head in order to catch what came out of it, than his eyes opened to twice their ordinary size with astonishment, while his throat moved vigorously in the act of swallowing. Then a smile and look of intense delight overspread his face, except, indeed, the mouth, which, being firmly fixed to the hole in the nut, could not take part in the expression; but he endeavoured to make up for this by winking at us excessively with his right eye. At length he stopped, and, drawing a long breath, exclaimed:

'Nectar! perfect nectar! I say, Jack, you're a Briton—the best fellow I ever met in my life.—Only taste that! said he, turning to me and holding the nut to my mouth. I immediately drank, and certainly I was much surprised at the delightful liquid that flowed copiously down my throat. It was extremely cool, and had a sweet taste, mingled with acid; in fact, it was the likest thing to lemonade I ever tasted, and was most refreshing. I handed the nut to Jack, who, after tasting it, said, 'Now, Peterkin, you unbeliever, I never saw or tasted a cocoa-nut in my life before, except those sold in shops at home; but I once read that the green nuts contain that stuff, and you see it is true!'

'And pray,' asked Peterkin, 'what sort of "stuff" does the ripe nut contain?'

'A hollow kernel,' answered Jack, 'with a liquid like milk in it; but it does not satisfy thirst so well as hunger. It is very wholesome food, I believe.'

'Meat and drink on the same tree!' cried Peterkin; 'washing in the sea, lodging on the ground—and all for nothing!

My dear boys, we're set up for life; it must be the ancient Paradise—hurrah!' and Peterkin tossed his straw hat in the air, and ran along the beach hallooing like a madman with delight.

We had now come to the point of rocks on which the ship had struck, but did not find a single article, although we searched carefully among the coral rocks, which at this place jutted out so far as nearly to join the reef that encircled the island. Just as we were about to return, however, we saw something black floating in a little cove that had escaped our observation. Running forward, we drew it from the water, and found it to be a long, thick leather boot, such as fishermen at home wear; and a few paces farther on we picked up its fellow. We at once recognized these as having belonged to our captain, for he had worn them during the whole of the storm. My first thought on seeing them was that our dear captain had been drowned; but Jack soon put my mind more at rest on that point, by saying that if the captain had been drowned with the boots on, he would certainly have been washed ashore along with them, and that he had no doubt whatever he had kicked them off while in the sea, that he might swim more easily.

Peterkin immediately put them on, but they were so large that, as Jack said, they would have done for boots, trousers, and vest too. I also tried them, but they were much too large in the feet for me; so we handed them to Jack, and as they fitted him as if they had been made for him, he consented at last to keep them.

It was beginning to grow dark when we returned to our encampment; so we put off our visit to the top of a hill till next day, and employed the light that yet remained in cutting down a quantity of boughs and the broad leaves of a tree of which none of us knew the name. With these we erected a sort of rustic bower, in which we meant to pass the night. There was no absolute necessity for this, because the air of our island was so genial and balmy that we could have slept quite well without any shelter; but we were so little used to sleeping in the open air, that we did not quite relish the idea of lying down without any covering over us; besides our bower would shelter us from the night-dews or rain, if any should happen to fall. Having strewed the floor with leaves and dry grass, we bethought ourselves of supper.

But it now occurred to us, for the first time, that we had no means of making a fire.

'Now, there's a fix!—what shall we do?' said Peterkin, while we both turned our eyes to Jack, to whom we always looked in our difficulties. Jack seemed not a little perplexed.

'There are flints enough, no doubt, on the beach,' said he, 'but they are of no use at all without a steel. However, we must try.' So saying, he went to the beach, and soon returned with two flints. On one of these he placed the tinder, and endeavoured to ignite it; but it was with great difficulty that a very small spark was struck out of the flints, and the tinder, being a bad, hard piece, would not catch. He then tried the bit of hoop iron, which would not strike fire at all; and after that the back of the axe, with no better success. During all these trials Peterkin sat with his hands in his pockets, gazing with a most melancholy visage at our comrade, his face growing longer and more miserable at each successive failure.

'Oh, I have it!' he cried, starting up at last: 'the spy-glass —the big glass at the end is a burning-glass!'

'You forget that we have no sun,' said I.

Peterkin was silent. In his sudden recollection of the telescope he had quite overlooked the absence of the sun.

'Ah, boys, I've got it now!' exclaimed Jack, rising and cutting a branch from a neighbouring bush, which he stripped of its leaves. 'I recollect seeing this done once at home. Hand me the bit of whip-cord.' With the cord and branch Jack soon formed a bow. Then he cut a piece, about three inches long, off the end of a dead branch, which he pointed at the two ends. Round this he passed the cord of the bow, and placed one end against his chest, which was protected from its point by a chip of wood; the other point he placed against the bit of tinder, and then began to saw vigorously with the bow, just as a blacksmith does with his drill while boring a hole in a piece of iron. In a few seconds the tinder began to smoke; in less than a minute it caught fire, and in less than a quarter of an hour we were drinking our lemonade and eating cocoa-nuts round a fire that would have roasted an entire sheep, while the smoke, flames, and sparks flew up among the broad leaves of the over-hanging palm trees, and cast a warm glow upon our leafy bower.

CHAPTER V

What a joyful thing it is to awaken, on a fresh glorious morning, and find the rising sun staring into your face with dazzling brilliancy! When I awoke on the morning after the shipwreck, I found myself in the most delightful condition; and as I lay on my back upon my bed of leaves, gazing up through the branches of the cocoa-nut trees into the clear blue sky, and watched the few fleecy clouds that passed slowly across it, my heart expanded more and more with an exulting the like of which I had never felt before.

Just at that moment I was attracted by the sight of a very small parrot, which Jack afterwards told me was called a paro-quet. It was seated on a twig that overhung Peterkin's head, and I was speedily lost in admiration of its bright green plum-age, which was mingled with other gay colours. While I looked I observed that the bird turned its head slowly from side to side and looked downwards, first with the one eye and then with the other. On glancing downwards I observed that Peterkin's mouth was wide open, and that this remarkable bird was look-ing into it. Suddenly it bent down its head and uttered a loud scream in his face. This awoke him, and, with a cry of surprise, he started up, while the foolish bird flew precipitately away.

'Oh, you monster!' cried Peterkin, shaking his fist at the bird. Then he yawned, and rubbed his eyes, and asked what o'clock it was.

I smiled at this question, and answered that, as our watches were at the bottom of the sea, I could not tell, but it was a little past sunrise.

Peterkin now began to remember where we were. As he looked up into the bright sky, and snuffed the scented air, his eyes glistened with delight, and he uttered a faint 'Hurrah!' and yawned again. Then he gazed slowly round, till, observing the calm sea through an opening in the bushes, he started suddenly up as if he had received an electric shock, uttered a vehement shout, flung off his garments, and, rushing over the white sands, plunged into the water. The cry awoke Jack, who rose on his elbow with a look of grave surprise; but this was followed by a quiet smile of intelligence on seeing Peterkin in the water. With an energy that he only gave way to in moments of excitement, Jack bounded to his feet, threw off his clothes, shook back his hair, and, with a lion-like spring, dashed over the sands and plunged into the sea with such force as quite to envelop Peterkin in a shower of spray. Jack was a remarkably good swimmer and diver, so that after his plunge we saw no sign of him till he suddenly emerged, with a cry of joy, a good many yards out from the shore. I, too, hastily threw off my garments, for I was really a good swimmer, and diver as well.

While Peterkin enjoyed himself in the shallow water and in running along the beach, Jack and I swam out into the deep water, and occasionally dived for stones. I shall never forget my surprise and delight on first beholding the bottom of the sea. The water within the reef was as calm as a pond; and, as there was no wind, it was quite clear, from the surface to the bottom, so that we could see down easily even at a depth of twenty or thirty yards. When Jack and I dived in shallower water, we expected to have found sand and stones, instead of which we found ourselves in what appeared really to be an enchanted garden. The whole of the bottom of the lagoon, as we called the calm water within the reef, was covered with coral of every shape, size, and hue. Some portions were formed like large mushrooms; others appeared like the brain of a man, having stalks or necks attached to them; but the most common kind was a species of branching coral, and some portions were of a lovely pale pink colour, others pure white. Among this there grew large quantities of sea-weed of the richest hues imaginable, and of the most graceful forms; while innumerable fishes—blue, red, yellow, green, and striped—sported in and out amongst the flower-beds of this submarine garden, and did not appear to be at all afraid of our approaching them.

On darting to the surface for breath, after our first dive, Jack and I rose close to each other.

'Did you ever in your life, Ralph, see anything so lovely?' said Jack, as he flung the spray from his hair.

'Never,' I replied. 'It appears to me like fairy realms. I can scarcely believe that we are not dreaming.'

'Dreaming!' cried Jack; 'do you know, Ralph, I'm half tempted to think that we really are dreaming. But if so, I am resolved to make the most of it, and dream another dive; so here goes—down again, my boy!'

We took the second dive together, and kept beside each other while under water; and I was greatly surprised to find that we could keep down much longer than I ever recollect having done in our own seas at home. I believe that this was owing to the heat of the water, which was so warm that we afterwards found we could remain in it for two and three hours at a time. When Jack reached the bottom, he grasped the coral stems, and crept along on his hands and knees, peeping under the sea-weed and among the rocks. I observed him also pick up one or two large oysters, and retain them in his grasp, as if he meant to take them up with him, so I also gathered a few. Suddenly he made a grasp at a fish with blue and yellow stripes on its back, and actually touched its tail, but did not catch it. At this he turned towards me and attempted to smile; but no sooner had he done so than he sprang like an arrow to the surface, where, on following him, I found him gasping and coughing, and spitting water from his mouth. In a few minutes he recovered, and we both turned to swim ashore.

'I declare, Ralph,' said he, 'that I actually tried to laugh under water.'

'So I saw,' I replied; 'and I observed that you very nearly caught that fish by the tail. It would have done capitally for breakfast if you had.'

'Breakfast enough here,' said he, holding up the oysters, as we landed and ran up the beach.—'Hallo, Peterkin! here you are, boy. Split open these fellows while Ralph and I put on our clothes. They'll agree with the cocoa-nuts excellently, I have no doubt.'

'I'm very glad that our prospect of breakfast is so good,' said I, 'for I'm very hungry.'

'Here then, stop your mouth with that, Ralph,' said Peterkin, holding a large oyster to my lips. I opened my mouth and swallowed it in silence, and really it was remarkably good.

We now set ourselves earnestly about our preparations for spending the day. We had no difficulty with the fire this morning, as our burning-glass was an admirable one; and while we roasted a few oysters and ate our cocoa-nuts, we held a long conversation about our plans for the future. What those plans were, and how we carried them into effect, the reader shall see hereafter.

CHAPTER VI

Our first care, after breakfast, was to place the few articles we possessed in the crevice of a rock at the farther end of a small cave which we discovered near our encampment. This cave, we hoped, might be useful to us afterwards as a storehouse. Then we cut two large clubs off a species of very hard tree which grew near at hand. One of these was given to Peterkin, the other to me, and Jack armed himself with the axe. We took these precautions because we purposed to make an excursion to the top of the mountains of the interior, in order to obtain a better view of our island. Of course we knew not what dangers might befall us by the way, so thought it best to be prepared.

Having completed our arrangements and carefully extinguished our fire, we sallied forth and walked a short distance along the sea-beach, till we came to the entrance of a valley, through which flowed a rivulet. Here we turned our backs on the sea and struck into the interior.

The prospect that burst upon our view on entering the valley was truly splendid. On either side of us there was a gentle rise in the land, which thus formed two ridges, about a mile apart on each side of the valley. These ridges—which, as well as the low grounds between them, were covered with trees and shrubs of the most luxuriant kind—continued to recede inland for about two miles, when they joined the foot of a small mountain. This hill rose rather abruptly from the head of the valley, and was covered to the top with trees, except on one particular spot near the left shoulder, where was a bare and rocky place of a broken and savage character. Beyond this hill we could not see, and we therefore directed our course up the banks of the rivulet towards the foot of it, intending to climb to the top, should that be possible.

Jack, being the wisest and boldest among us, took the lead, carrying the axe on his shoulder. Peterkin, with his enormous club, came second, as he said he should like to be in a position to defend me if any danger should threaten. I brought up the rear, but, having been more taken up with the wonderful and curious things I saw at starting than with thoughts of possible danger, I had very foolishly left my club behind me. Although, as I have said, the trees and bushes were very luxuriant, they were not so thickly crowded together as to hinder our progress among them. We were able to wind in and out, and to follow the banks of the stream quite easily, although, it is true, the height and thickness of the foliage prevented us from seeing far ahead. But sometimes a jutting-out rock on the hillsides afforded us a position whence we could enjoy the romantic view and mark our progress towards the base of the hill. I was particularly struck, during the walk, with the richness of the undergrowth in most places, and recognized many berries and plants that resembled those of my native land, especially a tall, elegantly formed fern, which emitted an agreeable perfume. There were several kinds of flowers, too, but I did not see so many of these as I should have expected in such a climate. We also saw a great variety of small birds of bright plumage, and many paroquets similar to the one that awoke Peterkin so rudely in the morning.

Thus we advanced to the foot of the hill, without encountering anything to alarm us, except, indeed, once, when we were passing close under a part of the hill which was hidden from our view by the broad leaves of the banana trees, which grew in great luxuriance in that part. Jack was just preparing to force his way through this thicket, when we were startled and arrested by a strange pattering or rumbling sound which appeared to us quite different from any of the sounds we had heard during the previous part of our walk.

'Hallo!' cried Peterkin, stopping short and grasping his club with both hands, 'what's that?'

Neither of us replied; but Jack seized his axe in his right hand, while with the other he pushed aside the broad leaves and endeavoured to peer amongst them.

'I can see nothing,' he said, after a short pause. 'I think it——'

Again the rumbling sound came, louder than before, and we all sprang back and stood on the defensive. For myself, having forgotten my club, and not having taken the precaution to cut another, I buttoned my jacket, doubled my fists, and threw myself into a boxing attitude. I must say, however, that I felt uneasy; and my companions afterwards confessed that their thoughts at this moment had been instantly filled with all they had ever heard or read of wild beasts and savages, torturings at the stake, roasting alive, and such horrible things. Suddenly the pattering noise increased with tenfold violence. It was followed by a fearful crash among the bushes, which was rapidly repeated, as if some gigantic animal were bounding towards us. In another moment an enormous rock came crashing through the shrubbery, followed by a cloud of dust and small stones, and flew close past the spot where we stood, carrying bushes and young trees along with it.

On examining the spot more narrowly, we found that it lay close to the foot of a very rugged precipice, from which stones of various sizes were tumbling at intervals. Indeed the numerous fragments lying scattered all around might have suggested the cause of the sound, had we not been too suddenly alarmed to think of anything.

We now resumed our journey, resolving that, in our future excursions into the interior, we would be careful to avoid this dangerous precipice.

Soon afterwards we arrived at the foot of the hill, and prepared to ascend it. Here Jack made a discovery which caused us all very great joy. This was a tree of a remarkably beautiful appearance, which Jack confidently declared to be the celebrated bread-fruit tree.

'Is it celebrated?' inquired Peterkin, with a look of great simplicity.

'It is,' replied Jack.

'That's odd, now,' rejoined Peterkin; 'I never heard of it before.'

'Then it's not so celebrated as I thought it was,' returned Jack, quietly squeezing Peterkin's hat over his eyes; 'but listen, you ignorant boobie! and hear of it now.'

Peterkin readjusted his hat, and was soon listening with as much interest as myself, while Jack told us that this tree is one of the most valuable in the islands of the south; that it bears two, sometimes three, crops of fruit in the year; that the fruit is very like wheaten bread in appearance, and that it constitutes the principal food of many of the islanders.

'So,' said Peterkin, 'we seem to have everything ready to our hands in this wonderful island—lemonade ready bottled in nuts, and loaf-bread growing on the trees!'

'Moreover,' continued Jack, 'the bread-fruit tree affords a capital gum, which serves the natives for pitching their canoes; the bark of the young branches is made by them into cloth; and of the wood, which is durable and of a good colour, they build their houses. So you see we have no lack of material here to make us comfortable, if we are only clever enough to use it.'

'But are you quite sure that that's it?' asked Peterkin.

'Quite sure,' replied Jack; 'for I remember the description well. I am sorry I have forgotten the descriptions of many other trees which I am sure we have seen to-day. So you see, Peterkin, I'm not up to everything yet.'

'Never mind, Jack,' said Peterkin, with a grave, patronizing expression of countenance, patting his tall companion on the shoulder—'never mind, Jack; you know a good deal for your age. You're a clever boy, sir—a promising young man; and if you only go on as you have begun, sir, you will——'

The end of this speech was suddenly cut short by Jack tripping up Peterkin's heels and tumbling him into a mass of thick shrubs, where, finding himself comfortable, he lay still, basking in the sunshine, while Jack and I examined the bread-fruit tree.

We were much struck with the deep, rich green colour of

(H 840)

its broad leaves, which were twelve or eighteen inches long, deeply indented, and of a glossy smoothness, like the laurel. The fruit, with which it was loaded, was nearly round, and about six inches in diameter, with a rough rind, marked with lozenge-shaped divisions. It was of various colours, from light pea-green to brown and rich yellow. Jack said that the yellow was the ripe fruit. We afterwards found that most of the fruit-trees on the island were evergreens, and that we might, when we wished, pluck the blossom and the ripe fruit from the same tree. The bark of the tree was rough and light-coloured; the trunk was about two feet in diameter, and about twenty feet high, up to the lowest branches, where it branched into a beautiful and umbrageous head. We noticed that the fruit hung in clusters of twos and threes on the branches; but as we were anxious to get to the top of the hill, we refrained from attempting to pluck any at that time.

We were now cheered by our good fortune, and with light and active steps clambered up the steep sides of the hill. On reaching the summit, a new and if possible a grander prospect met our gaze. We found that this was not the highest part of the island, but that another hill lay beyond, with a wide valley between it and the one on which we stood. After gazing our fill we pushed down the hillside, crossed the valley, and soon began to ascend the second mountain. It was clothed with trees nearly to the top, but the summit was bare, and in some places broken.

While on our way up we came to an object which filled us with much interest. This was the stump of a tree that had evidently been cut down with an axe! So we were not the first who had viewed this beautiful isle. The hand of man had been at work there before us. It now began to occur to us again that perhaps the island was inhabited, although we had not seen any traces of man until now; but a second glance at the stump convinced us that we had no more reason to think so now than formerly; for the surface of the wood was quite decayed, and partly covered with fungus, so that it must have been cut many years ago.

'Perhaps,' said Peterkin, 'some ship or other has touched here long ago for wood, and only taken one tree.'

We did not think this likely, however, because, in such

2   (H 840)

circumstances, the crew of a ship would cut wood of small size, and near the shore, whereas this was a large tree and stood near the top of the mountain.

'I can't understand it,' said Jack, scratching the surface of the stump with his axe. 'I can only suppose that the savages have been here and cut it for some purpose known only to themselves. But, hallo! what have we here?'

As he spoke, Jack began carefully to scrape away the moss and fungus from the stump, and soon laid bare three distinct traces of marks, as if some inscription or initials had been cut thereon. But although the traces were distinct, beyond all doubt, the exact form of the letters could not be made out. Jack thought they looked like J.S., but we could not be certain. They had apparently been carelessly cut, and long exposure to the weather had so broken them up that we could not make out what they were. So, as the day was advancing, we proceeded and quickly reached the top of the mountain.

We found this to be the highest point of the island, and from it we saw our kingdom lying, as it were, like a map around us. It consisted of two mountains: the one we guessed at 500 feet; the other, on which we stood, at 1000. Between these a rich beautiful valley crossed the island from one end to the other, being high in the middle and sloping on each side towards the sea. On the side farthest from where we had been wrecked, the large mountain sloped gradually towards the sea; but although, when viewed at a glance, it had thus a regular sloping appearance, a more careful observation showed that it was broken up into a multitude of very small vales, or rather dells and glens, inter-mingled with little rugged spots and small but abrupt precipices here and there, with rivulets tumbling over their edges and wandering down the slopes in little white streams, sometimes glistening among the broad leaves of the bread-fruit and cocoa-nut trees, or hiding altogether beneath the rich underwood. At the base of this mountain lay a narrow bright green plain which terminated abruptly at the shore. On the other side of the island, whence we had come, stood the smaller hill, at the foot of which diverged three valleys; one being that which we had ascended, with a smaller vale on each side of it, and separated from it by the two ridges before mentioned. In these

smaller valleys there were no streams, but they were clothed
with the same luxuriant vegetation.

The diameter of the island seemed to be about ten miles,
and as it was almost circular in form, its circumference must
have been thirty miles—perhaps a little more, if allowance be
made for the numerous bays and indentations of the shore.
The entire island was belted by a beach of pure white sand,
and the coral reef completely encircled the island; its distance
varied, in some places being a mile from the beach, in others a
few hundred yards, the average being about half a mile. The
reef lay very low, and the spray of the surf broke quite over it
in many places. This surf never ceased its roar, for however
calm the weather might be, there is always a gentle swaying
motion in the great Pacific, which, although scarce noticeable
out at sea, reaches the shore at last in a huge billow. There
were three narrow openings in the reef: one opposite each end
of the valley which I have described as crossing the island; the
other opposite our own valley, which we afterwards named the
Valley of the Wreck. At each of these openings the reef rose
into two small green islets, covered with bushes and having
one or two cocoa-nut palms on each. These islets were very
singular, and appeared as if planted expressly for the purpose
of marking the channel into the lagoon. Our captain was
making for one of these openings the day we were wrecked,
and would have reached it too, I doubt not, had not the rudder
been torn away. Within the lagoon were several low coral
islands, just opposite our encampment; and immediately
beyond these, out at sea, lay about half a dozen other islands, at
various distances, from half a mile to ten miles—all of them, as
far as we could discern, smaller than ours and apparently
uninhabited. They seemed to be low coral islands, raised but
little above the sea, yet covered with cocoa-nut trees.

All this we noted, and a great deal more, while we sat on the
top of the mountain. After we had satisfied ourselves we prepared to return; and again we discovered traces of the presence
of man. These were a pole or staff and one or two pieces of
wood which had been squared with an axe. They were,
however, much decayed, and had evidently not been touched
for many years.

CHAPTER VII

For several days after the excursion related in the last chapter we did not wander far from our encampment, but gave ourselves up to forming plans for the future and making our present abode comfortable.

There were various causes that induced this state of comparative inaction. In the first place, although everything around us was so delightful, and we could without difficulty obtain all that we required for our bodily comfort, we did not quite like the idea of settling down here for the rest of our lives, far away from our friends and our native land. To set energetically about preparations for a permanent residence seemed so like making up our minds to saying adieu to home and friends for ever, that we shrank from it, and put off our preparations, for one reason and another, as long as we could.

During this time, however, we had not been altogether idle. We made several experiments in cooking the cocoa-nut, most of which did not improve it. Then we removed our goods, and took up our abode in the cave, but found the change so bad that we returned gladly to the bower. Besides this, we bathed very frequently, and talked a great deal; at least Jack and Peterkin did—I listened. Among other useful things, Jack, who was ever the most active and diligent, converted about three inches of the hoop iron into an excellent knife. First he beat it quite flat with the axe. Then he made a rude handle, and tied the hoop iron to it with our piece of whip-cord, and ground it to an edge on a piece of sandstone. When it was finished he used it to shape a better handle, to which he fixed it with a strip of his handkerchief—a cotton one ornamented with a Union Jack and sixteen portraits of Lord Nelson. However, the whip-cord, thus set free, was used by Peterkin as a fishing-line. He merely tied a piece of oyster to the end of it. This the fish were allowed to swallow, and then they were pulled quickly ashore. But as the line was very short and we had no boat, the fish we caught were exceedingly small.

One day Peterkin came up from the beach, where he had

been angling, and said in a very cross tone, 'I'll tell you what, Jack, I'm not going to be humbugged with catching such contemptible things any longer. I want you to swim out with me on your back, and let me fish in deep water!'

'Dear me, Peterkin!' replied Jack, 'I had no idea you were taking the thing so much to heart, else I would have got you out of that difficulty long ago. Let me see,'—and Jack looked down at a piece of timber on which he had been labouring, with a peculiar gaze of abstraction which he always assumed when trying to invent or discover anything.

'What say you to building a boat?' he inquired, looking up hastily.

'Take far too long,' was the reply; 'can't be bothered waiting. I want to begin at once!'

Again Jack considered. 'I have it!' he cried. 'We'll fell a large tree and launch the trunk of it in the water, so that when you want to fish you've nothing to do but to swim out to it.'

'Would not a small raft do better?' said I.

'Much better; but we have no ropes to bind it together with. Perhaps we may find something hereafter that will do as well, but in the meantime let us try the tree.'

This was agreed on, so we started off to a spot not far distant, where we knew of a tree that would suit us, which grew near the water's edge. As soon as we reached it Jack threw off his coat, and, wielding the axe with his sturdy arms, hacked and hewed at it for a quarter of an hour without stopping. Then he paused, and while he sat down to rest I continued the work. Then Peterkin made a vigorous attack on it, so that when Jack renewed his powerful blows, a few minutes' cutting brought it down with a terrible crash.

'Hurrah! now for it,' cried Jack; 'let us off with its head.'

So saying he began to cut through the stem again, at about six yards from the thick end. This done, he cut three strong, short poles or levers from the stout branches, with which to roll the log down the beach into the sea; for, as it was nearly two feet thick at the large end, we could not move it without such helps. With the levers, however, we rolled it slowly into the sea.

Having been thus successful in launching our vessel, we next shaped the levers into rude oars or paddles, and then attempted to embark. This was easy enough to do; but after seating ourselves astride the log, it was with the utmost difficulty we kept it from rolling round and plunging us into the water. Not that we minded that much; but we preferred, if possible, to fish in dry clothes. To be sure, our trousers were necessarily wet, as our legs were dangling in the water on each side of the log; but as they could be easily dried, we did not care. After half an hour's practice, we became expert enough to keep our balance pretty steadily. Then Peterkin laid down his paddle, and having baited his line with a whole oyster, dropped it into deep water.

'Now then, Jack,' said he, 'be cautious; steer clear o' that sea-weed. There! that's it; gently now, gently. I see a fellow at least a foot long down there, coming to—ah! that's it. Oh bother! he's off.'

'Did he bite?' said Jack, urging the log onwards a little with his paddle.

'Bite? ay! He took it into his mouth, but the moment I began to haul he opened his jaws and let it out again.'

'Let him swallow it next time,' said Jack, laughing at the melancholy expression of Peterkin's visage.

'There he's again,' cried Peterkin, his eyes flashing with excitement. 'Look out! Now then! No! Yes! No! Why, the brute *won't* swallow it!'

'Try to haul him up by the mouth, then,' cried Jack. 'Do it gently.'

A heavy sigh and a look of blank despair showed that poor Peterkin had tried and failed again.

'Never mind, lad,' said Jack, in a voice of sympathy; 'we'll move on, and offer it to some other fish.' So saying, Jack plied his paddle; but scarcely had he moved from the spot, when a fish with an enormous head and a little body darted from under a rock and swallowed the bait at once.

'Got him this time—that's a fact!' cried Peterkin, hauling in the line. 'He's swallowed the bait right down to his tail, I declare. Oh, what a thumper!'

As the fish came struggling to the surface, we leaned forward to see it, and overbalanced the log. Peterkin threw his arms round the fish's neck, and in another instant we were all floundering in the water!

A shout of laughter burst from us as we rose to the surface like three drowned rats, and seized hold of the log. We soon recovered our position, and sat more warily, while Peterkin secured the fish, which had well-nigh escaped in the midst of our struggles. It was little worth having, however; but, as Peterkin remarked, it was better than the smouts he had been catching for the last two or three days; so we laid it on the log before us, and having re-baited the line, dropped it in again for another.

Now, while we were thus intent upon our sport, our attention was suddenly attracted by a ripple on the sea, just a few yards away from us. Peterkin shouted to us to paddle in that direction, as he thought it was a big fish, and we might have a chance of catching it. But Jack, instead of complying, said, in a deep, earnest tone of voice, which I never before heard him use:

'Haul up your line, Peterkin; seize your paddle; quick—it's a shark!'

The horror with which we heard this may well be imagined, for it must be remembered that our legs were hanging down in the water, and we could not venture to pull them up without upsetting the log. Peterkin instantly hauled up the line, and grasping his paddle, exerted himself to the utmost, while we also did our best to make for shore. But we were a good way off, and the log being, as I have before said, very heavy, moved but slowly through the water. We now saw the shark quite distinctly swimming round and round us, its sharp fin every now and then protruding above the water. From its active and unsteady motions, Jack knew it was making up its mind to attack us, so he urged us vehemently to paddle for our lives, while he himself set us the example. Suddenly he shouted, 'Look out! there he comes!' and in a second we saw the monstrous fish dive close under us, and turn half over on his side. But we all made a great commotion with our paddles, which no doubt frightened it away for that time, as we saw it immediately after circling round us as before.

'Throw the fish to him,' cried Jack, in a quick, suppressed voice; 'we'll make the shore in time yet if we can keep him off for a few minutes.'

Peterkin stopped one instant to obey the command, and then plied his paddle again with all his might. No sooner had the fish fallen on the water than we observed the shark to sink. In another second we saw its white breast rising; for sharks always turn over on their sides when about to seize their prey, their mouths being not at the point of their heads like those of other fish, but, as it were, under their chins. In another moment his snout rose above the water; his wide jaws, armed with a terrific double row of teeth, appeared. The dead fish was engulfed, and the shark sank out of sight. But Jack was mistaken in supposing that it would be satisfied. In a very few minutes it returned to us, and its quick motions led us to fear that it would attack us at once.

'Stop paddling,' cried Jack suddenly. 'I see it coming up behind us. Now, obey my orders *quickly*. Our lives may depend on it. Ralph, Peterkin, do your best to *balance* the log. Don't look out for the shark. Don't glance behind you. Do nothing but balance the log.'

Peterkin and I instantly did as we were ordered, being only too glad to do anything that afforded us a chance or a hope of escape, for we had implicit confidence in Jack's courage and wisdom. For a few seconds, that seemed long minutes to my mind, we sat thus silently; but I could not resist glancing backward, despite the orders to the contrary. On doing so, I saw Jack sitting rigid like a statue, with his paddle raised, his lips compressed, and his eyebrows bent over his eyes, which glared savagely from beneath them down into the water. I also saw the shark, to my horror, quite close under the log, in the act of darting towards Jack's foot. I could scarce suppress a cry on beholding this. In another moment the shark rose. Jack drew his leg suddenly from the water, and threw it over the log. The monster's snout rubbed against the log as it passed, and revealed its hideous jaws, into which Jack instantly plunged the paddle, and thrust it down its throat. So violent was this act that Jack rose to his feet in performing it; the log was thereby rolled completely over, and we were once more plunged into the water. We all rose, spluttering and gasping in a moment.

'Now, then, strike out for shore,' cried Jack.—'Here, Peterkin, catch hold of my collar, and kick out with a will.'

Peterkin did as he was desired, and Jack struck out with such force that he cut through the water like a boat; while I, being free from all encumbrance, succeeded in keeping up with him. As we had by this time drawn pretty near to the shore, a few minutes more sufficed to carry us into shallow water; and finally, we landed in safety, though very much exhausted, and not a little frightened by our terrible adventure.

CHAPTER VIII

Our encounter with the shark was the first great danger that had befallen us since landing on this island, and we felt very seriously affected by it, especially when we considered that we had so often unwittingly incurred the same danger before while bathing. We were now forced to take to fishing again in the shallow water, until we should succeed in constructing a raft. What troubled us most, however, was, that we were compelled to forego our morning swimming excursions. We did, indeed, continue to enjoy our bathe in the shallow water, but Jack and I found that one great source of our enjoyment was gone, when we could no longer dive down among the beautiful coral groves at the bottom of the lagoon. We had come to be so fond of this exercise, and to take such an interest in watching the formations of coral and the gambols of the many beautiful fish amongst the forests of red and green sea-weed, that we had become quite familiar with the appearance of the fish and the localities that they chiefly haunted. We had also become expert divers. But we made it a rule never to stay long under water at a time. Jack told me that to do so often was bad for the lungs, and, instead of affording us enjoyment, would ere long do us a serious injury. So we never stayed at the bottom as long as we might have done, but came up frequently to the top for fresh air, and dived down again immediately. I used often to wonder how poor Peterkin would have liked to be with us, so one day prevailed on him to try to go down with us. But although a brave boy in every other way, Peterkin was very nervous in the water, and it was with difficulty we got him to consent to be taken down, for he could never have managed to push himself down to the bottom without assistance. But no sooner had we pulled him down a yard or so into the deep clear water, than he began to struggle and kick violently; so we were forced to let him go, when he rose out of the water like a cork, gave a loud gasp and a frightful roar, and struck out for the land with the utmost possible haste.

Now all this pleasure we were to forego, and when we thought thereon, Jack and I felt very much depressed in our spirits. As, however, a man's difficulties usually set him upon devising methods to overcome them, whereby he often discovers better things than those he may have lost, so this our difficulty induced us to think of searching for a large pool among the rocks, where the water should be deep enough for diving, yet so surrounded by rocks as to prevent sharks from getting at us. And such a pool we afterwards found, which proved to be very much better than our most sanguine hopes anticipated. It was situated not more than ten minutes' walk from our camp, and was in the form of a small deep bay or basin, the entrance to which, besides being narrow, was so shallow that no fish so large as a shark could get in, at least not unless he should be a remarkably thin one.

Inside of this basin, which we called our Water Garden, the coral formations were much more wonderful, and the sea-weed plants far more lovely and vividly coloured, than in the lagoon itself. And the water was so clear and still, that, although very deep, you could see the minutest object at the bottom. Besides this, there was a ledge of rock which overhung the basin at its deepest part, from which we could dive pleasantly. During these excursions of ours we began to get an insight into the manners and customs of its inhabitants, and make discoveries of wonderful things, the like of which we never before conceived. Among other things, we were deeply interested with the operations of the little coral insect which, I was informed by Jack, is supposed to have entirely constructed many of the numerous islands in the Pacific Ocean. And certainly, when we considered the great reef which these insects had formed round the island on which we were cast, and observed their ceaseless activity in building their myriad cells, it did at first seem as if this might be true. But more of this hereafter.

I also became much taken up with the manners and appearance of the anemones, and star-fish, and crabs, and sea-urchins, and such-like creatures; and was not content with watching those I saw during my dives in the Water Garden, but I must needs scoop out a hole in the coral rock close to it, which I filled with salt water, and stocked with sundry specimens of anemones and shell-fish, in order to watch more closely how they were in the habit of passing their time. Our burning-glass also now became a great treasure to me, as it enabled me to magnify, and so to perceive more clearly the forms and actions of these curious creatures of the deep.

Having now got ourselves into a very comfortable condition, we began to talk of a project which we had long had in contemplation—namely, to travel entirely round the island; in order, first, to ascertain whether it contained any other productions which might be useful to us; and, second, to see whether there might be any place more convenient and suitable for our permanent residence than that on which we were now encamped. Not that we were in any degree dissatisfied with it; on the contrary, we entertained quite a home-feeling to our bower and its neighbourhood; but if a better place did exist, there was no reason why we should not make use of it. At any rate, it would be well to know of its existence.

We had much earnest talk over this matter. But Jack proposed that, before undertaking such an excursion, we should supply ourselves with good defensive arms; for as we intended not only to go round all the shore, but to ascend most of the valleys, before returning home, we should be likely to meet in with, he would not say *dangers*, but at least with everything that existed on the island, whatever that might be.

'Besides,' said Jack, 'it won't do for us to live on cocoa-nuts and oysters always. No doubt they are very excellent in their way, but I think a little animal food now and then would be good for us; and as there are many small birds among the trees, it would be a capital plan to make bows and arrows, with which we could knock them over.'

'But,' said I, 'Jack, you cannot make three bows and arrows before to-morrow, and would it not be a pity to waste time, now that we have made up our minds to go on this expedition? Suppose that you make one bow and arrow for yourself, and we can take our clubs?'

'That's true, Ralph. The day is pretty far advanced, and I doubt if I can make even one bow before dark. To be sure, I might work by fire-light, after the sun goes down.'

We had, up to this time, been in the habit of going to bed with the sun, as we had no pressing call to work o' nights; and, indeed, our work during the day was usually hard enough —what between fishing, and improving our bower, and diving in the Water Garden, and rambling in the woods; so that, when night came, we were usually very glad to retire to our beds. But now that we had a desire to work at night, we felt a wish for candles.

'Won't a good blazing fire give you light enough?' inquired Peterkin.

'Yes, replied Jack, 'quite enough; but then it will give us a great deal more than enough of heat in this warm climate of ours.'

'True,' said Peterkin; 'I forgot that. It will roast us.'

'The fact is,' said Jack, 'I've been thinking over this subject before. There is a certain nut growing in these islands which is called the candle-nut, because the natives use it instead of candles, and I know all about it, and how to prepare it for burning——'

'Then why don't you do it?' interrupted Peterkin. 'Why have you kept us in the dark so long, you vile philosopher?'

'Because,' said Jack, 'I have not seen the tree yet, and I'm not sure that I should know either the tree or the nuts if I did see them. You see, I forget the description. I believe the nut is about the size of a walnut; and I think that the leaves are white, but I am not sure.'

'Eh! ha! hum!' exclaimed Peterkin, 'I saw a tree answering that description this very day.'

'Did you?' cried Jack. 'Is it far from this?'

'No, not half a mile.'

'Then lead me to it,' said Jack, seizing his axe.

In a few minutes we were all three pushing through the underwood of the forest, headed by Peterkin.

We soon came to the tree in question, which, after Jack had closely examined it, we concluded must be the candle-nut tree. Its leaves were of a beautiful silvery white, and formed a fine contrast to the dark-green foliage of the surrounding trees. We immediately filled our pockets with nuts, after which Jack said:

'Now, Peterkin, climb that cocoa-nut tree and cut me one of the long branches.'

This was soon done, but it cost some trouble, for the stem was very high, and as Peterkin usually pulled nuts from the younger trees, he was not much accustomed to climbing the high ones. The leaf or branch was a very large one, and we were surprised at its size and strength. Viewed from a little distance, the cocoa-nut tree seems to be a tall, straight stem, without a single branch except at the top, where there is a tuft of feathery-looking leaves, that seem to wave like soft plumes in the wind But when we saw one of these leaves or branches at our feet, we found it to be a strong stalk, about fifteen feet long, with a number of narrow, pointed leaflets ranged alternately on each side. But what seemed to us the most wonderful thing about it was a curious substance resembling cloth, which was wrapped round the thick end of the stalk, where it had been cut from the tree. Peterkin told us that he had the greatest difficulty in separating the branch from the stem on account of this substance, as it was wrapped quite round the tree, and round all the other branches, thus forming a strong support to the large leaves while exposed in high winds. When I call this substance cloth I do not exaggerate. Indeed, with regard to all the things I saw during my eventful career in the South Seas, I have been exceedingly careful not to exaggerate, or in any way to mislead or deceive my readers. This cloth, I say, was remarkably like to coarse brown cotton cloth. It had a seam or fibre down the centre of it, from which diverged other fibres, about the size of a bristle. There were two layers of these fibres, very long and tough, the one layer crossing the other obliquely, and the whole was cemented together with a still finer fibrous and adhesive substance. When we regarded it attentively, we could with difficulty believe that it had not been woven by human hands. This remarkable piece of cloth we stripped carefully off, and found it to be above two feet long by a foot broad, and we carried it home with us as a great prize.

Jack now took one of the leaflets, and, cutting out the central spine or stalk, hurried back with it to our camp. Having made a small fire, he baked the nuts slightly, and then peeled off the husks. After this he wished to bore a hole in them, which, not having anything better at hand at the time, he did with the point of our useless pencil-case. Then he strung them on the cocoa-nut spine, and on putting a light to the topmost nut, we found to our joy that it burned with a clear, beautiful flame; upon seeing which, Peterkin sprang up and danced round the fire for at least five minutes in the excess of his satisfaction.

'Now, lads,' said Jack, extinguishing our candle, 'the sun will set in an hour, so we have no time to lose. I shall go and cut a young tree to make my bow out of, and you had better each of you go and select good strong sticks for clubs, and we'll set to work at them after dark.'

So saying he shouldered his axe and went off, followed by Peterkin, while I took up the piece of newly discovered cloth, and fell to examining its structure. So engrossed was I in this that I was still sitting in the same attitude and occupation when my companions returned.

'I told you so!' cried Peterkin, with a loud laugh—'Oh Ralph, you're incorrigible. See, there's a club for you. I was sure, when we left you looking at that bit of stuff, that we would find you poring over it when we came back, so I just cut a club for you as well as for myself.'

'Thank you, Peterkin,' said I. 'It was kind of you to do that, instead of scolding me for a lazy fellow, as I confess I deserve.'

'Oh, as to that,' returned Peterkin, 'I'll blow you up yet,

if you wish it; only it would be of no use if I did, for you're a perfect mule!'

As it was now getting dark we lighted our candle, and placing it in a holder made of two crossing branches, inside of our bower, we seated ourselves on our leafy beds and began to work.

'I intend to appropriate the bow for my own use,' said Jack, chipping the piece of wood he had brought with his axe. 'I used to be a pretty fair shot once. But what's that you're doing?' he added, looking at Peterkin, who had drawn the end of a long pole into the tent, and was endeavouring to fit a small piece of the hoop iron to the end of it.

'I'm going to enlist into the Lancers,' answered Peterkin. 'You see, Jack, I find the club rather an unwieldy instrument for my delicately formed muscles, and I flatter myself I shall do more execution with a spear.'

'Well, if length constitutes power, said Jack, 'you'll certainly be invincible.'

The pole which Peterkin had cut was full twelve feet long, being a very strong but light and tough young tree, which merely required thinning at the butt to be a serviceable weapon.

'That's a very good idea,' said I.

'Which—this?' inquired Peterkin, pointing to the spear.

'Yes,' I replied.

'Humph!' said he; 'you'd find it a pretty tough and matter-of-fact idea if you had it stuck through your gizzard, old boy!'

'I mean the idea of making it is a good one,' said I, laughing. 'And, now I think of it, I'll change my plan too. I don't think much of a club, so I'll make a sling out of this piece of cloth. I used to be very fond of slinging, ever since I read of David slaying Goliath the Philistine, and I was once thought to be expert at it.'

So I set to work to manufacture a sling. For a long time we all worked very busily without speaking. At length Peterkin looked up. 'I say, Jack, I'm sorry to say I must apply to you for another strip of your handkerchief, to tie on this rascally head with. It's pretty well torn at any rate, so you won't miss it.'

While we were thus engaged, we were startled by a distant but most strange and horrible cry. It seemed to come from the sea, but was so far away that we could not clearly distinguish its precise direction. Rushing out of our bower, we hastened down to the beach and stayed to listen. Again it came quite loud and distinct on the night air—a, prolonged, hideous cry, something like the braying of an ass. The moon had risen, and we could see the islands in and beyond the lagoon quite plainly, but there was no object visible to account for such a cry. A strong gust of wind was blowing from the point whence the sound came, but this died away while we were gazing out to sea.

'What can it be?' said Peterkin, in a low whisper, while we all involuntarily crept closer to each other.

'Do you know,' said Jack, 'I have heard that sound twice before, but never so loud as to-night. Indeed it was so faint that I thought I must have merely fancied it, so, as I did not wish to alarm you, I said nothing about it.'

We listened for a long time for the sound again, but as it did not come, we returned to the bower and resumed our work.

'Very strange,' said Peterkin, quite gravely. 'Do you believe in ghosts, Ralph?'

'No,' I answered, 'I do not. Nevertheless I must confess that strange sounds, such as we have just heard, make me feel a little uneasy.'

'What say you to it, Jack?'

'I neither believe in ghosts nor feel uneasy,' he replied. 'I certainly can't imagine what *that* sound is; but I'm quite sure I shall find out before long, and if it's a ghost I'll—I'll——'

'Eat it,' cried Peterkin.

'Yes, I'll eat it! Now, then, my bow and two arrows are finished; so if you're ready we'd better turn in.'

By this time Peterkin had thinned down his spear and tied an iron point very cleverly to the end of it; I had formed a sling, the lines of which were composed of thin strips of the cocoa-nut cloth, plaited; and Jack had made a stout bow, nearly five feet long, with two arrows, feathered with two or three large plumes which some bird had dropped.

The string of the bow was formed of our piece of whip-cord,

part of which, as he did not like to cut it, was rolled round the bow.

Although thus prepared for a start on the morrow, we thought it wise to exercise ourselves a little in the use of our weapons before starting, so we spent the whole of the next day in practising. And it was well we did so, for we found that our arms were very imperfect, and that we were far from perfect in the use of them. First, Jack found that the bow was much too strong, and he had to thin it. Also the spear was much too heavy, and so had to be reduced in thickness, although nothing would induce Peterkin to have it shortened. My sling answered very well, but I had fallen so much out of practice that my first stone knocked off Peterkin's hat, and narrowly missed making a second Goliath of him. However, after having spent the whole day in practice, we began to improve. Peterkin soon handled his spear well, and could run full tilt at a cocoa-nut, and hit it with great precision once out of every five times.

Although we were much fatigued, we examined and repaired our arms ere we lay down to rest, in order that we might be ready to set out at daylight on the following morning.

CHAPTER IX

Scarcely had the sun shot its first ray across the bosom of the broad Pacific, when Jack sprang to his feet, and, hallooing in Peterkin's ear to awaken him, ran down the beach to take his customary dip in the sea. We did not bathe that morning in our Water Garden, but, to save time, refreshed ourselves in the shallow water just opposite the bower. Our breakfast was also dispatched without loss of time, and in less than an hour all our preparations for the journey were completed.

In addition to his ordinary dress, Jack tied a belt of cocoa-nut cloth round his waist, into which he thrust the axe. I also put on a belt to carry a short cudgel; for, as Jack remarked, the sling would be of little use if we should chance to come to close quarters with any wild animal. As for Peterkin, notwithstanding that he carried such a long and frightful-looking spear over his shoulder, we could not prevail on him to leave his club behind; 'for,' said he, 'a spear at close quarters is not worth a button.'

We did not consider it necessary to carry food with us, as we knew that wherever we went we should be certain to fall in with cocoa-nut trees; having which, we were amply supplied, as Peterkin said, with meat and drink and pocket handkerchiefs! I took the precaution, however, to put the burning-glass into my pocket, lest we should want fire.

Peterkin walked along the sands between us. We had two ways of walking together about our island. When we travelled through the woods, we always did so in single file, as by this method we advanced with greater facility, the one treading in the other's footsteps. In such cases Jack always took the lead, Peterkin followed, and I brought up the rear. But when we travelled along the sands, which extended almost in an unbroken line of glistening white round the island, we marched abreast, as we found this method more sociable, and every way more pleasant. Jack, being the tallest, walked next the sea, and Peterkin marched between us, as by this arrangement either of us could talk to him or he to us, while if Jack and I happened to wish to converse together, we could do so over Peterkin's head.

We were now fairly started. Half a mile's walk brought us round a bend in the land which shut out our bower from view, and for some time we advanced at a brisk pace without speaking, though our eyes noted everything, in the woods, on the shore, or in the sea, that was interesting. After passing the ridge of land that formed one side of our valley—the Valley of the Wreck—we beheld another small vale lying before us in all the luxuriant loveliness of tropical vegetation. We had, indeed, seen it before from the mountain-top, but we had no idea that it would turn out to be so much more lovely when we were close to it. We were about to commence the exploration of this valley, when Peterkin stopped us, and directed our attention to a very remarkable appearance in advance along the shore.

'What's yon, think you?' said he, levelling his spear, as if he expected an immediate attack from the object in question, though it was full half a mile distant.

As he spoke, there appeared a white column above the rocks, as if of steam or spray. It rose upwards to a height of several feet, and then disappeared. Had this been near the sea, we would not have been so greatly surprised, as it might in that case have been the surf, for at this part of the coast the coral reef approached so near to the island that in some places it almost joined it. There was therefore no lagoon between, and the heavy surf of the ocean beat almost up to the rocks. But this white column appeared about fifty yeards inland. The rocks at the place were rugged, and they stretched across the sandy beach into the sea. Scarce had we ceased expressing our surprise at this sight, when another column flew upwards for a few seconds, not far from the spot where the first had been seen, and disappeared; and so, at long, irregular intervals, these sights recurred. We were now quite sure that the columns were watery or composed of spray, but what caused them we could not guess, so we determined to go and see.

In a few minutes we gained the spot, which was rugged and precipitous, and damp with the falling of the spray. We had much ado to pass over dry-shod. The ground also was full of holes. While we stood anxiously waiting for the reappearance of these waterspouts, we heard a low, rumbling sound near us, which quickly increased to a gurgling and hissing noise, and a moment afterwards a thick spout of water burst upwards from a hole in the rock, and spouted into the air with much violence, and so close to where Jack and I were standing that it nearly touched us. We sprang to one side, but not before a cloud of spray descended, and drenched us both to the skin.

Peterkin, who was standing farther off, escaped with a few drops, and burst into an uncontrollable fit of laughter on beholding our miserable plight.

'Mind your eye!' he shouted eagerly, 'there goes another!' The words were scarcely out of his mouth when there came up a spout from another hole, which served us exactly in the same manner as before.

Peterkin now shrieked with laughter; but his merriment was abruptly put to a stop by the gurgling noise occurring close to where he stood.

'Where'll it spout this time, I wonder?' he said, looking about with some anxiety, and preparing to run. Suddenly there came a loud hiss or snort; a fierce spout of water burst up between Peterkin's legs, blew him off his feet, enveloped him in its spray, and hurled him to the ground. He fell with so much violence that we feared he must have broken some of his bones, and ran anxiously to his assistance; but fortunately he had fallen on a clump of tangled herbage, in which he lay sprawling in a most deplorable condition.

It was now our turn to laugh; but as we did not know when or where the next spout might arise, we helped him up hastily and hurried from the spot.

'What's to be done now?' inquired Peterkin ruefully.

'Best make a fire and dry ourselves,' replied Jack.

'And here is material ready to our hand,' said I, picking up a dried branch of a tree, as we hurried up to the woods.

In about an hour our clothes were again dried. While they were hanging up before the fire, we walked down to the beach, and soon observed that these curious spouts took place immediately after the fall of a huge wave, never before it; and, moreover, that the spouts did not take place excepting when the wave was an extremely large one. From this we concluded that there must be a subterraneous channel in the rock into which the water was driven by the larger waves, and finding no way of escape except through these small holes, was forced up through them. At any rate, we could not conceive any other reason for these strange waterspouts, and this seemed a simple and probable explanation.

'I say, Ralph, what's that in the water? is it a shark?' said Jack, just as we were about to quit the place.

I immediately ran to the overhanging ledge of rock, from which he was looking down into the sea, and bent over it. There I saw a very faint pale object of a greenish colour, which seemed to move slightly while I looked at it.

'It's like a fish of some sort,' said I.

'Hallo, Peterkin!' cried Jack, 'fetch your spear; here's work for it.'

But when we tried to reach the object, the spear proved to be too short.

'There now,' cried Peterkin, 'you were always telling me it was too long.'

Jack now drove the spear forcibly towards the object, and let go his hold; but although it seemed to be well aimed, he must have missed, for the handle soon rose again; and when the spear was drawn up, there was the pale green object in exactly the same spot, slowly moving its tail.

'Very odd,' said Jack.

But although it was undoubtedly very odd, and although Jack and all of us plunged the spear at it repeatedly, we could neither hit it nor drive it away, so we had to continue our journey without discovering what it was.

CHAPTER X

Our examination of the little valley proved to be altogether satisfactory. We found in it not only trees similar to those we had already seen in our own valley, but also one or two others of a different kind. We also discovered a peculiar vegetable, which Jack concluded must certainly be that of which he had read as being very common among the South Sea islanders, and which was named *taro*. Also we found a large supply of yams, and another root like a potato in appearance. As these were all quite new to us, we regarded our lot as most fortunate, in being thus cast on an island which was so well stored with all the necessaries of life. Long afterwards we found out that this island of ours was no better in these respects than thousands of other islands in those seas. Indeed, many of them were much richer and more productive; but that did not render us the less grateful for our present good fortune. We put some of these roots in our pockets, intending to use them for supper; of which more hereafter. We also saw many beautiful birds, and traces of some four-footed animal. Meanwhile the sun began to descend, so we returned to the shore, and pushed on round the spouting rocks into the next valley. This was that valley of which I have spoken as running across the entire

island. It was by far the largest and most beautiful that we had
yet looked upon.

Now, while we were gazing around us in silent admiration,
Jack uttered an exclamation of surprise, and pointing to an
object a little to one side of us, said:

'That's a banyan tree.'

'And what's a banyan tree?' inquired Peterkin, as we walked
towards it.

'A very curious one, as you shall see presently,' replied
Jack. 'It is called the *aoa* here, if I recollect rightly, and has
a wonderful peculiarity about it. What an enormous one it is,
to be sure!'

'*It!*' repeated Peterkin; 'why, there are dozens of banyans
here! What do you mean by talking bad grammar, Jack?'

'There is but one tree here of this kind,' returned Jack,
'as you will perceive if you will examine it.' And, sure enough,
we did find that what we had supposed was a forest of trees
was in reality only one. Its bark was of a light colour, and had
a shining appearance, the leaves being lance-shaped, small,
and of a beautiful pea-green. But the wonderful thing about it
was, that the branches, which grew out from the stem hori-
zontally, sent down long shoots or fibres to the ground, which,
taking root, had themselves become trees, and were covered
with bark like the tree itself. Many of these shoots had descended from the branches at various distances, and supported
them as if on natural pillars, some of which were so large and
strong that it was not easy at first to distinguish the shoot from
the parent stem. The shoots were of all sizes and in all states
of advancement, from the pillars we have just mentioned to
small cords which hung down and were about to take root,
and thin brown threads still far from the ground, which swayed
about with every motion of wind. In short, it seemed to us
that, if there were only space afforded to it, this single tree
would at length cover the whole island.

Shortly after this we came upon another remarkable tree,
which, as its peculiar formation afterwards proved extremely
useful to us, merits description. It was a splendid chestnut,
but its proper name Jack did not know. However, there were
quantities of fine nuts upon it, some of which we put in our

pockets. But its stem was the wonderful part of it. It rose to about twelve feet without a branch, and was not of great thickness: on the contrary, it was remarkably slender for the size of the tree; but, to make up for this, there were four or five wonderful projections in this stem, which I cannot better describe than by asking the reader to suppose that five planks of two inches thick and three feet broad had been placed round the trunk of the tree, with their *edges* closely fixed to it, from the ground up to the branches, and that these planks had been covered over with the bark of the tree and incorporated with it. In short, they were just natural buttresses, without which the stem could not have supported its heavy and umbrageous top. We found many chestnut trees of all sizes, chiefly on the banks of the stream.

While we were examining a small tree of this kind, Jack chipped a piece off a buttress with his axe, and found the wood to be firm and easily cut. He then struck the axe into it with all his force, and very soon split it off, close to the tree, first, however, having cut it across transversely above and below. By this means he satisfied himself that we could now obtain short planks, as it were all ready sawn, of any size and thickness that we desired; which was a very great discovery indeed, perhaps the most important we had yet made.

We now wended our way back to the coast, intending to encamp near the beach, as we found that the mosquitos were troublesome in the forest. On our way we could not help admiring the birds which flew and chirped around us. Among them we observed a pretty kind of paroquet, with a green body, a blue head, and a red breast; also a few beautiful turtle-doves, and several flocks of wood-pigeons. The hues of many of these birds were extremely vivid—bright green, blue, and scarlet being the prevailing tints. We made several attempts throughout the day, both with the bow and the sling, to bring down one of them, but we invariably missed, although once or twice we were very near hitting. As evening drew on, however, a flock of pigeons flew past. I slung a stone into the midst of them at a venture, and had the good fortune to kill one. We were startled, soon after, by a loud, whistling noise above our heads; and on looking up, saw a flock of wild-ducks making for the coast. We watched these, and observing where they alighted, followed them up until we came upon a most lovely blue lake, not more than two hundred yards long, embosomed in verdant trees. Its placid surface, which reflected every leaf and stem as if in a mirror, was covered with various species of wild-ducks, feeding among the sedges, and with broad-leaved water-plants, while numerous birds like water-hens ran to and fro on the margin. These with one accord flew away the instant we made our appearance.

Now, as we neared the shore, Jack and I said we would go a little out of our way to see if we could procure one of those ducks; so, directing Peterkin to go straight to the shore and kindle a fire, we separated, promising to rejoin him speedily. But we did not find the ducks, although we made a diligent search for half an hour. We were about to retrace our steps, when we were arrested by one of the strangest sights that we had yet beheld.

Just in front of us, at the distance of about ten yards, grew a superb tree, which certainly was the largest we had yet seen on the island. Its trunk was at least five feet in diameter, with a smooth grey bark; above this the spreading branches were clothed with light green leaves, amid which were clusters of bright yellow fruit, so splendid as to weight down the boughs. This fruit seemed to be of the plum species, of an oblong form, and a good deal larger than the magnum bonum plum. The ground at the foot of the tree was thickly strewn with the fallen fruit, in the midst of which lay sleeping, in every possible attitude, at least twenty hogs of all ages and sizes, apparently quite surfeited with a recent banquet.

Jack and I could scarce restrain our laughter as we gazed at these fat, ill-looking animals while they lay groaning and snoring heavily amid the remains of their supper.

'Now, Ralph,' said Jack, in a low whisper, 'put a stone in your sling—a good big one—and let fly at that fat fellow with his back toward you. I'll try to put an arrow into yon little pig.'

'Don't you think we had better put them up first?' I whispered; 'it seems cruel to kill them while asleep.'

'If I wanted *sport*, Ralph, I would certainly set them up;

but as we only want *pork*, we'll let them lie. Besides, we're not sure of killing them; so, fire away.'

Thus admonished, I slung my stone with so good aim that it went bang against the hog's flank as if against the head of a drum; but it had no other effect than that of causing the animal to start to its feet, with a frightful yell of surprise, and scamper away. At the same instant Jack's bow twanged, and the arrow pinned the little pig to the ground by the ear.

'I've missed, after all,' cried Jack, darting forward with uplifted axe, while the little pig uttered a loud squeal, tore the arrow from the ground, and ran away with it, along with the whole drove, into the bushes and disappeared, though we heard them screaming long afterwards in the distance.

'That's very provoking, now,' said Jack, rubbing the point of his nose.

'Very,' I replied, stroking my chin.

'Well, we must make haste and rejoin Peterkin,' said Jack. 'It's getting late.' And without further remark we threaded our way quickly through the woods towards the shore.

When we reached it, we found wood laid out, the fire lighted and beginning to kindle up, with other signs of preparation for our encampment, but Peterkin was nowhere to be found. We wondered very much at this; but Jack suggested that he might have gone to fetch water; so he gave a shout to let him know that we had arrived, and sat down upon a rock, while I threw off my jacket, and seized the axe, intending to split up one or two billets of wood. But I had scarce moved from the spot when, in the distance, we heard a most appalling shriek, which was followed up by a chorus of yells from the hogs, and a loud hurrah.

'I do believe,' said I, 'that Peterkin has met with the hogs.'

'Hurrah!' shouted Peterkin in the distance.

We turned hastily towards the direction whence the sound came, and soon descried Peterkin walking along the beach towards us with a little pig tranfixed on his spear.

'Well done, my boy!' exclaimed Jack, slapping him on the shoulder when he came up; 'you're the best shot amongst us.'

'Look here, Jack!' cried Peterkin, as he disengaged the animal from his spear. 'Do you recognize that hole?' said he, pointing to the pig's ear; 'and are you familiar with this arrow, eh?'

'Well, I declare!' said Jack.

'Of course you do,' interrupted Peterkin; 'but, pray, restrain your declarations at this time, and let's have supper, for I'm uncommonly hungry, I can tell you; and it's no joke to charge a whole herd of swine with their great-grandmother bristling like a giant porcupine at the head of them!'

We now set about preparing supper; and, truly, a good display of viands we made, when all was laid out on a flat rock in the light of the blazing fire. There was, first of all, the little pig; then there was the taro-root, and the yam, and the potato, and six plums; and, lastly, the wood-pigeon. To these Peterkin added a bit of sugar-cane, which he had cut from a little patch of that plant which he had found not long after separating from us; 'and,' said he, 'the patch was square, which convinces me it must have been planted by man.'

'Very likely,' replied Jack. 'From all we have seen, I'm inclined to think that some of the natives must have lived here long ago.'

We found no small difficulty in making up our minds how we were to cook the pig. None of us had ever cut up one before, and we did not know exactly how to begin; besides, we had nothing but the axe to do it with, our knife having been forgotten. At last Jack started up and said:

'Don't let us waste more time talking about it, boys.— Hold it up, Peterkin. There, lay the hind leg on this block of wood—so;' and he cut it off, with a large portion of the haunch, at a single blow of the axe. 'Now the other—that's it.' And having thus cut off the two hind legs, he made several deep gashes in them, thrust a sharp-pointed stick through each, and stuck them up before the blaze to roast. The wood-pigeon was then split open, quite flat, washed clean in salt water, and treated in a similar manner. While these were cooking, we scraped a hole in the sand and ashes under the fire, into which we put our vegetables, and covered them up.

Having eaten our fill, not forgetting to finish off with a plum, we laid ourselves comfortably down to sleep upon a couch of branches, under the overhanging ledge of a coral rock.

CHAPTER XI

When we awoke on the following morning, we found that the sun was already a good way above the horizon, so I came to the conclusion that a heavy supper is not conducive to early rising. Nevertheless, we felt remarkably strong and well, and ready for breakfast. First, however, we had our morning bathe, which refreshed us greatly.

We had not advanced on our journey much above a mile or so, and were just beginning to feel the pleasant glow that accompanies vigorous exercise, when, on turning a point that revealed to us a new and beautiful cluster of islands, we were suddenly arrested by the cry which had so alarmed us a few nights before.

On hearing the sound, Peterkin hastily threw forward his spear.

'Now, what can it be?' said he, looking round at Jack. 'I tell you what it is: if we are to go on being pulled up in a constant state of horror and astonishment, as we have been for the last week, the sooner we're out o' this island the better, notwithstanding the yams and lemonade, and pork and plums!'

Peterkin's remark was followed by a repetition of the cry, louder than before.

'It comes from one of these islands,' said Jack.

'It must be the ghost of a jackass, then,' said Peterkin, 'for I never heard anything so like.'

We all turned our eyes towards the cluster of islands, where, on the largest, we observed curious objects moving on the shore.

'Soldiers they are—that's flat!' cried Peterkin, gazing at them in the utmost amazement.

And, in truth, Peterkin's remark seemed to me to be correct; for, at the distance from which we saw them, they appeared to be an army of soldiers. There they stood, rank and file, in lines and in squares, marching and counter-marching, with blue coats and white trousers. While we were looking at them, the dreadful cry came again over the water, and Peterkin suggested that it must be a regiment sent out to massacre the natives in cold blood. At this remark Jack laughed and said:

'Why, Peterkin, they are penguins!'

'Penguins?' repeated Peterkin.

'Ay, penguins, Peterkin, penguins—nothing more or less than big sea-birds, as you shall see one of these days, when we pay them a visit in our boat.'

'So, then, our dreadful yelling ghosts and our murdering army of soldiers,' remarked Peterkin, 'have dwindled down to penguins—big sea-birds! Very good. Then I propose that we continue our journey as fast as possible, lest our island should be converted into a dream before we get completely round it.'

As we continued on our way, I pondered over this new discovery, and the singular appearance of these birds, of which Jack could only give us a very slight and vague account; and I began to long to commence at our boat, in order that we might go and inspect them more narrowly. But by degrees these thoughts left me, and I began again to be taken up with the peculiarities of the country which we were passing through.

The second night we passed in a manner somewhat similar to the first, at about two-thirds of the way round the island, as we calculated, and we hoped to sleep on the night following at our bower. I will not here note so particularly all that we said and saw during the course of this second day, as we did not make any further discoveries of great importance. The shore along which we travelled, and the various parts of the woods through which we passed, were similar to those which have been already treated of.

We found several more droves of hogs in the woods, but abstained from killing any of them, having more than sufficient for our present necessities. We saw also many of their footprints in this neighbourhood. Among these we also observed the footprints of a smaller animal, which we examined with much care, but could form no certain opinion as to them. Peterkin thought they were those of a little dog, but Jack and I thought differently. We became very curious on this matter, the more so that we observed these footprints to lie scattered about in one locality, as if the animal which had made them was wandering round about in a very irregular manner, and without any object in view. Early in the forenoon of our third day we observed these footprints to be much more numerous than ever, and in one particular spot they diverged off into the woods in a regular beaten track, which was, however, so closely beset with bushes that we pushed through it with difficulty. We had now become so anxious to find out what animal this was and where it went to, that we determined to follow the track, and, if possible, clear up the mystery. Peterkin said, in a bantering tone, that he was sure it would be cleared up, as usual, in some frightfully simple way, and prove to be no mystery at all!

The beaten track seemed much too large to have been formed by the animal itself, and we concluded that some larger animal had made it, and that the smaller one made use of it. But everywhere the creeping plants and tangled bushes crossed our path, so that we forced our way along with some difficulty. Suddenly, as we came upon an open space, we heard a faint cry, and observed a black animal standing in the track before us.

'A wild-cat!' cried Jack, fitting an arrow to his bow, and discharging it so hastily that he missed the animal, and hit the earth about half a foot to one side of it. To our surprise the wild-cat did not fly, but walked slowly towards the arrow, and snuffed at it.

'That's the most comical wild-cat I ever saw!' cried Jack.

'It's a tame wild-cat, I think,' said Peterkin, levelling his spear to make a charge.

'Stop!' cried I, laying my hand on his shoulder; 'I do believe the poor beast is blind. See, it strikes against the branches as it walks along. It must be a very old one;' and I hastened towards it.

'Only think,' said Peterkin, with a suppressed laugh, 'of a superannuated wild-cat!'

We now found that the poor cat was not only blind, or nearly so, but extremely deaf, as it did not hear our footsteps until we were quite close behind it. Then it sprang round, and putting up its back and tail, while the black hair stood all on end, uttered a hoarse mew and a fuff.

'Poor thing!' said Peterkin, gently extending his hand, and endeavouring to pat the cat's head. 'Poor pussy; chee, chee, chee; puss, puss, puss; cheetie pussy!'

No sooner did the cat hear these sounds than all signs of anger fled, and advancing eagerly to Peterkin, it allowed itself to be stroked, and rubbed itself against his legs, purring loudly all the time, and showing every symptom of the most extreme delight.

'It's no more a wild-cat than I am!' cried Peterkin, taking it in his arms; 'it's quite tame.—Poor pussy, cheetie pussy!'

We now crowded around Peterkin, and were surprised, and, to say truth, a good deal affected, by the sight of the poor animal's excessive joy. It rubbed its head against Peterkin's cheek, licked his chin, and thrust its head almost violently into his neck, while it purred more loudly than I ever heard a cat purr before, and appeared to be so much overpowered by its feelings, that it occasionally mewed and purred almost in the same breath. Such demonstrations of joy and affection led us at once to conclude that this poor cat must have known man before, and we conjectured that it had been left either accidentally or by design on the island many years ago. While we were fondling the cat and talking about it, Jack glanced round the open space in the midst of which we stood.

'Hallo!' exclaimed he; 'this looks something like a clearing. The axe has been at work here. Just look at these tree-stumps.'

We now turned to examine these, and without doubt we found trees that had been cut down here and there, also stumps and broken branches; all of which, however, were completely covered over with moss, and bore evidence of having been in this condition for some years. No human footprints were to be seen either on the track or among the bushes, but those of the cat were found everywhere. We now determined to follow up the track as far as it went, and Peterkin put the cat down; but it seemed to be so weak, and mewed so very pitifully, that he took it up again and carried it in his arms, where in a few minutes it fell sound asleep.

About ten yards farther on, the felled trees became more numerous, and the track, diverging to the right, followed for a short space the banks of a stream. Suddenly we came to a spot where once must have been a rude bridge, the stones of which were scattered in the stream, and those on each bank entirely covered over with moss. In silent surprise and expectancy we continued to advance, and, a few yards farther on, beheld, under the shelter of some bread-fruit trees, a small hut. I cannot hope to convey to my readers a very correct idea of the feelings that affected us on witnessing this unexpected sight. We stood for a long time in silent wonder, for there was a deep and most melancholy stillness about the place that quite overpowered us; and when we did at length speak, it was in whispers, as if we were surrounded by some awful or supernatural influence. Even Peterkin's voice, usually so quick and lively, was hushed now; for there was a dreariness about this silent, lonely, uninhabited hut—so strange in its appearance so far away from the usual dwellings of man, so old, decayed, and deserted in its aspect—that fell upon our spirits like a thick cloud, and blotted out as with a pall the cheerful sunshine that had filled us since the commencement of our tour round the island.

The hut was rude and simple in its construction. It was not more than twelve feet long by ten feet broad, and about seven or eight feet high. It had one window, or rather a small frame in which a window might perhaps once have been, but which was now empty. The door was exceedingly low, and formed of rough boards, and the roof was covered with broad cocoa-nut and plantain leaves. But every part of it was in a state of the utmost decay. Moss and green matter grew in spots all over it. The wood-work was quite perforated with holes; the roof had nearly fallen in, and appeared to be prevented from doing so altogether by the thick matting of creeping plants and the interlaced branches which years of neglect had allowed to cover it almost entirely; while the thick, luxuriant branches of the bread-fruit and other trees spread above it, and flung a deep, sombre shadow over the spot, as if to guard it from the heat and the light of day. We conversed long and in whispers about this strange habitation ere we ventured to approach it; and when at length we did so, it was with feelings of awe.

At first Jack endeavoured to peep in at the window, but in the gloom he could not clearly discern objects; so we lifted the latch and pushed open the door. We observed that the latch was made of iron, and almost eaten away with rust. In the like condition were also the hinges, which creaked as the door swung back. On entering, we stood still and gazed around us, while we were much impressed with the dreary stillness of the room. But what we saw there surprised and shocked us not a little. There was no furniture in the apartment save a little wooden stool and an iron pot, the latter almost eaten through with rust. In the corner farthest from the door was a low bedstead, on which lay two skeletons, embedded in a little heap of dry dust. With beating hearts we went forward to examine them. One was the skeleton of a man, the other that of a dog, which was extended close beside that of the man, with its head resting on his bosom.

Now we were very much concerned about this discovery, and could scarce refrain from tears on beholding these sad remains. After some time, we began to talk about what we had seen, and to examine in and around the hut, in order to discover some clue to the name or history of this poor man, who had thus died in solitude, with none to mourn his loss save his cat and his faithful dog. But we found nothing—neither a book nor a scrap of paper. We found, however, an old axe and the decayed remnants of what appeared to have been clothing. But none of these things bore marks of any kind; and, indeed, they were so much decayed as to convince us that they had lain in the condition in which we found them for many years.

This discovery now accounted to us for the tree-stump at the top of the mountain with the initials cut on it; also for the patch of sugar-cane and other traces of man which we had met with in the course of our rambles over the island. And we were much saddened by the reflection that the lot of this poor wanderer might possibly be our own, after many years' residence on the island, unless we should be rescued by the visit of some vessel or the arrival of natives. Having no clue whatever to account for the presence of this poor human being in such a lonely spot, we fell to conjecturing what could have brought him here. I was inclined to think that he must have been a shipwrecked sailor, whose vessel had been lost here, and all the crew been drowned except himself and his dog and cat. But Jack thought it more likely that he had run away from his vessel, and had taken the dog and cat to keep him company.

While we were thinking on these things, and examining into everything about the room, we were attracted by an exclamation from Peterkin.

'I say, Jack,' said he, 'here is something that will be of use to us.'

'What is it?' said Jack, hastening across the room.

'An old pistol,' replied Peterkin, holding up the weapon, which he had just pulled from under a heap of broken wood and rubbish that lay in a corner.

'That, indeed, might have been useful,' said Jack, examining it, 'if we had any powder; but I suspect the bow and the sling will prove more serviceable.'

'True, I forgot that,' said Peterkin; 'but we may as well take it with us, for the flint will serve to strike fire with when the sun does not shine.'

After having spent more than an hour at this place without discovering anything of further interest, Peterkin took up the old cat, which had lain very contentedly asleep on the stool whereon he had placed it, and we prepared to take our departure. In leaving the hut, Jack stumbled heavily against the door-post, which was so much decayed as to break across, and the whole fabric of the hut seemed ready to tumble about our ears. This put into our heads that we might as well pull it down, and so form a mound over the skeleton. Jack, therefore, with his axe, cut down the other door-post and brought the whole hut in ruins to the ground, and thus formed a grave for the poor recluse and his dog. Then we left the spot, having brought away the iron pot, the pistol, and the old axe.

During the rest of this day we pursued our journey, and examined the other end of the large valley, which we found to be much like the parts already described.

———

CHAPTER XII

Rest is sweet as well for the body as for the mind. Of rest
we stood much in need on our return home, and we found it
exceedingly sweet after completing the journey just related.
Our minds were exhausted in consequence of the many sur-
prises and frequent alarms; so that when we lay down on the
night of our return under the shelter of the bower, we fell
immediately into deep sleep. We slept all night and the whole
of the following day. When we awoke it was near sunset, and
we were all in such a state of lassitude that we merely rose to
swallow a mouthful of food. As Peterkin remarked, in the
midst of a yawn, we took breakfast at tea-time, and then went
to bed again, and lay till the following forenoon.

After this we arose very greatly refreshed, but much alarmed
lest we had lost count of a day. However, on consideration, we
came to the same opinion as to how long we had slept, and so
our minds were put at ease.

We now hastened to our Water Garden to enjoy a bathe,
and to see how did the animals which I had placed in the tank.
We found the garden more charming, pellucid, and inviting
than ever, and Jack and I plunged into its depth and gambolled
among its radiant coral groves, while Peterkin wallowed at the
surface, and tried occasionally to kick us as we passed below.

'Hallo! what's this?' cried Peterkin suddenly. 'I say, Ralph,
look here. There's one o' your crabs up to something
uncommon. It's performing the most remarkable operation
for a crab I ever saw—taking off its coat, I do believe, before
going to bed!'

We hastily stooped over the tank, and certainly were not a
little amused at the conduct of the crab. It was one of the
common small crabs, like to those that are found running about
everywhere on the coasts of England. While we gazed at it, we
observed its back to split away from the lower part of its body,
and out of the gap thus formed came a soft lump which moved
and writhed unceasingly. This lump continued to increase in
size until it appeared like a bunch of crab's legs; and, indeed,

such it proved to be, for the points of the toes were at length extricated from this hole in its back, the legs spread out; the body followed, and the crab walked away quite entire, even to the points of its nipper-claws, leaving a perfectly entire shell behind it, so that, when we looked, it seemed as though there were two complete crabs instead of one.

'Well!' exclaimed Peterkin, drawing a long breath, 'I've heard of a man jumping out of his skin, and sitting down in his skeleton in order to cool himself, but I never expected to see a crab do it!'

We were, in truth, amazed at this spectacle, and the more so when we observed that the new crab was larger than the crab that it came out of. It was also quite soft, but by next morning its skin had hardened into a good shell. We came thus to know that crabs grow in this way, and not by the growing of their shells.

For many days after this, while Peterkin and Jack were busily employed in building a boat out of the curious natural planks of the chestnut tree, I spent much of my time in examining with the burning-glass the marvellous operations that were constantly going on in my tank; but I refrain from setting down more particulars here, as I have still much to tell of the adventures that befell us while we remained on this island.

CHAPTER XIII

'Come, Jack,' cried Peterkin, one morning about three weeks after our return from our long excursion, 'let's be jolly to-day, and do something vigorous.'

'Well,' answered Jack, throwing down the axe with which he was just about to proceed towards the boat, 'if that's what you want, let's make an excursion to the waterspouts. The last one we had to do with tossed you up a considerable height; perhaps the next will send you higher, who knows, if you're at all reasonable or moderate in your expectations!'

'Jack, my dear boy,' said Peterkin gravely, 'you are really

becoming too fond of jesting. It's a thing I don't at all approve of, and if you don't give it up, I fear that we shall have to part.'

'Well, then, Peterkin,' replied Jack, with a smile, 'what would you have?'

'Have?' said Peterkin; 'I would have nothing. I didn't say I wanted to have; I said that I wanted to do.'

'By the bye,' said I, 'we have not yet discovered the nature of yon curious appearance that we saw near the waterspouts, on our journey round the island. Perhaps it would be well to go for that purpose.'

'Humph!' ejaculated Peterkin. 'I know the nature of it well enough.'

'What was it?' said I.

'It was of a mysterious nature to be sure!' said he, with a wave of his hand, while he rose from the log on which he had been sitting and buckled on his belt, into which he thrust his enormous club.

'Well, then, let us away to the water-spouts,' cried Jack, going up to the bower for his bow and arrows; 'and bring your spear, Peterkin. It may be useful.'

We now, having made up our minds to examine into this matter, sallied forth eagerly in the direction of the waterspout rocks, which, as I have before mentioned, were not far from our present place of abode. On arriving there we hastened down to the edge of the rocks and gazed over into the sea, where we observed the pale-green object still distinctly visible, moving its tail slowly to and fro in the water.

'Most remarkable!' said Jack.

'Exceeding curious!' said I.

'Beats everything!' said Peterkin.

'Now, Jack,' he added, 'you made such a poor figure in your last attempt to stick that object, that I would advise you to let me try it. If it has got a heart at all, I'll engage to send my spear right through the core of it; if it hasn't got a heart, I'll send it through the spot where its heart ought to be.'

'Fire away then, my boy,' replied Jack, with a laugh.

Peterkin immediately took the spear, poised it for a second or two above his head, then darted it like an arrow into the sea. Down it went straight into the centre of the green object, passed quite through it, and came up immediately afterwards, pure and unsullied, while the mysterious tail moved quietly as before!

'Now,' said Peterkin gravely, 'that brute is a heartless monster; I'll have nothing more to do with it.'

'I'm pretty sure now,' said Jack, 'that it is merely a phosphoric light; but I must say I'm puzzled at its staying always in that exact spot.'

I also was much puzzled, and inclined to think with Jack that it must be phosphoric light, of which luminous appearance we had seen much while on our voyage to these seas. 'But,' said I, 'there is nothing to hinder us from diving down to it, now that we are sure it is not a shark.'

'True,' returned Jack, stripping off his clothes; 'I'll go down, Ralph, as I'm better at diving than you are.—Now then, Peterkin, out o' the road!' Jack stepped forward, joined his hands above his head, bent over the rocks, and plunged into the sea. For a second or two the spray caused by his dive hid him from view; then the water became still, and we saw him swimming far down in the midst of the green object. Suddenly he sank below it, and vanished altogether from our sight! We gazed anxiously down at the spot where he had disappeared for nearly a minute expecting every moment to see him rise again for breath; but fully a minute passed, and still he did not reappear. Two minutes passed! and then a flood of alarm rushed in upon my soul, when I considered that, during all my acquaintance with him, Jack had never stayed under water more than a minute at a time; indeed, seldom so long.

For the next five minutes the intensity of my feelings almost bereft me of my senses. But I was recalled to myself by Peterkin seizing me by the shoulder and staring wildly into my face, while he exclaimed, 'Ralph, Ralph! perhaps he has only fainted. Dive for him, Ralph!'

It seemed strange that this did not occur to me sooner. In a moment I rushed to the edge of the rocks, and, without waiting to throw off my clothes, was on the point to spring into the waves, when I observed somthing black rising up through the green object. In another moment Jack's head rose to the surface, and he gave a wild shout, flinging back the spray from his locks, as was his wont after a dive. Now we were almost as much amazed at seeing him reappear, well and strong, as we had been at first at his non-appearance; for, to the best of our judgement, he had been nearly ten minutes under water.

'Now, lads,' said Jack, when we were composed enough to listen to him, 'yon green object is not a shark; it is a stream of light issuing from a cave in the rocks. Just after I made my dive, I observed that this light came from the side of the rock above which we are now sitting; so I struck out for it, and saw an opening into some place or other that appeared to be luminous within. For one instant I paused to think whether I ought to venture. Then I made up my mind, and dashed into it. For you see, Peterkin, although I take some time to tell this, it happened in the space of a few seconds, so that I knew I had wind enough in me to serve to bring me out o' the hole and up to the surface again. Well, I was just on the point of turning —for I began to feel a little uncomfortable in such a place— when it seemed to me as if there was a faint light right above me. I darted upwards, and found my head out of water. This relieved me greatly, for I now felt that I could take in air enough to enable me to return the way I came.

'At first I could scarcely see anything as I gazed around me, it was so dark; but gradually my eyes became accustomed to it, and I found that I was in a huge cave, part of the walls of which I observed on each side of me. The ceiling just above me was also visible, and I fancied that I could perceive beautiful glittering objects there; but the farther end of the cave was shrouded in darkness. While I was looking around me in great wonder, it came into my head that you two would think I was drowned; so I plunged down through the passage again in a great hurry, rose to the surface, and—here I am!'

When Jack concluded his recital of what he had seen in this remarkable cave, I could not rest satisfied till I had dived down to see it; which I did, but found it so dark that I could scarcely see anything. When I returned, we had a long conversation about it, during which I observed that Peterkin had a most lugubrious expression on his countenance.

'What's the matter, Peterkin?' said I.

'The matter?' he replied. 'It's all very well for you two

to be talking away like mermaids about the wonders of this cave, but you know I must be content to hear about it, while you are enjoying yourselves down there like mad dolphins. It's really too bad.'

'I'm very sorry for you, Peterkin, indeed I am,' said Jack, 'but we cannot help you. If you would only learn to dive——'

'Learn to fly, you might as well say!' retorted Peterkin, in a very sulky tone.

'If you would only consent to keep still,' said I, 'we would take you down with us in ten seconds.'

'Hum!' returned Peterkin; 'suppose a salamander was to propose to you "only to keep still", and he would carry you through a blazing fire in a few seconds, what would you say?'

We both laughed and shook our heads, for it was evident that nothing was to be made of Peterkin in the water. But we could not rest satisfied till we had seen more of this cave; so, after further consultation, Jack and I determined to try if we could take down a torch with us, and set fire to it in the cavern. This we found to be an undertaking of no small difficulty, but we accomplished it at last by the following means:— First, we made a torch of a very inflammable nature out of the bark of a certain tree. This we cut into strips, and, after twisting, cemented together with a kind of resin or gum, which we obtained from another tree. This, when prepared, we wrapped up in a great number of plies of cocoa-nut cloth, so that we were confident it could not get wet during the short time it should be under water. Then we took a small piece of the tinder, which we had carefully treasured up lest we should require it when the sun should fail us; also, we rolled up some dry grass and a few chips, which, with a little bow and drill like those described before, we made into another bundle, and wrapped up in cocoa-nut cloth. When all was ready we laid aside our garments, with the exception of our trousers, which, as we did not know what rough scraping against the rocks we might be subjected to, we kept on.

Then we advanced to the edge of the rocks, Jack carrying one bundle, with the torch, I the other, with the things for producing fire.

'Now don't weary for us, Peterkin, should we be gone some time,' said Jack; 'we'll be sure to return in half an hour at the very latest.'

We gained the interior of the submarine cave without difficulty, and, on emerging from the waves, supported ourselves for some time by treading water, while we held the two bundles above our heads. This we did in order to let our eyes become accustomed to the obscurity. Then, when we could see sufficiently, we swam to a shelving rock, and landed in safety. Having wrung the water from our trousers, and dried ourselves as well as we could under the circumstances, we proceeded to ignite the torch. This we accomplished without difficulty in a few minutes; and no sooner did it flare up than we were struck dumb with the wonderful objects that were revealed to our gaze. The roof of the cavern just above us seemed to be about ten feet high, but grew higher as it receded into the distance, until it was lost in darkness. It seemed to be made of coral, and was supported by massive columns of the same material. Immense icicles (as they appeared to us) hung from it in various places. These, however, were formed, not of ice, but of limestone, which seemed to flow in a liquid form towards the point of each, where it became solid. A good many drops fell, however, to the rock below, and these formed little cones, which rose to meet the points above. Some of them had already met, and thus we saw how the pillars were formed, which at first seemed to us as if they had been placed there by some human architect. As we advanced farther in, we saw that the floor was composed of the same material as the pillars, and presented the curious appearance of ripples, such as are formed on water when gently ruffled by the wind. There were several openings on either hand in the walls, that seemed to lead into other caverns; but these we did not explore at this time. We also observed that the ceiling was curiously marked in many places, as if it were the fretwork of a noble cathedral; and the walls, as well as the roof, sparkled in the light of our torch, and threw back gleams and flashes, as if they were covered with precious stones. Although we proceeded far into this cavern, we did not come to the end of it, and were obliged to return more speedily than we would otherwise have done, as our torch was nearly expended. We did not observe any openings in the roof, or any indications of places whereby light might enter; but near the entrance to the cavern stood an immense mass of pure white coral rock, which caught and threw back the little light that found an entrance through the cave's mouth, and thus produced the pale-green object which had first attracted our attention. We concluded, also, that the reflecting power of this rock was that which gave forth the dim light that faintly illumined the first part of the cave.

Before again diving through the passage we extinguished the small piece of our torch that remained, and left it in a dry spot; conceiving that we might possibly stand in need of it, if at any future time we should chance to wet our torch while diving into the cavern. As we stood for a few minutes after it was out, waiting till our eyes became accustomed to the gloom, we could not help remarking the deep, intense stillness and the unutterable gloom of all around us.

In a few seconds, however, we were panting on the rocks above, and receiving the congratulations of our friend Peterkin.

CHAPTER XIV

It was quite a relief to us to breathe the pure air and to enjoy the glad sunshine after our long ramble in the Diamond Cave, as we named it; for although we did not stay more than half an hour away, it seemed to us much longer. While we were dressing, and during our walk home, we did our best to satisfy the curiosity of poor Peterkin, who seemed to regret, with lively sincerity, his inability to dive.

There was no help for it, however, so we condoled with him as we best could. Had there been any great rise or fall in the tide of these seas, we might perhaps have found it possible to take him down with us at low water; but as the tide never rose or fell more than eighteen inches or two feet, this was impossible.

This peculiarity of the tide—its slight rise and fall—had not attracted our observation till some time after our residence on the island. Neither had we observed another curious circumstance until we had been some time there. This was the fact that the tide rose and fell with constant regularity, instead of being affected by the changes of the moon as in our own country, and as it is in most other parts of the world—at least in all those parts with which I am acquainted. Every day and every night, at twelve o'clock precisely, the tide is at the full; and at six o'clock every morning and evening it is ebb. I can speak with much confidence on this singular circumstance, as we took particular note of it, and never found it to alter. Of course, I must admit, we had to guess the hour of twelve midnight, and I think we could do this pretty correctly; but in regard to twelve noon we are quite positive, because we easily found the highest point that the sun reached in the sky by placing ourselves at a certain spot whence we observed the sharp summit of a cliff resting against the sky just where the sun passed.

And while I am on this subject—namely, the tides—I may here remark on another curious natural phenomenon. We found that there was little or no twilight in this island. We had a distinct remembrance of the charming long twilight at home, and when we first landed, we used to sit down on some rocky point or eminence, at the close of our day's work, to enjoy the evening breeze; but no sooner had the sun sunk below the horizon than all became suddenly dark. This rendered it necessary that we should watch the sun when we happened to be out hunting; for to be suddenly left in the dark while in the woods was very perplexing, as, although the stars shone with great beauty and brilliancy, they could not pierce through the thick umbrageous boughs that interlaced above our heads.

But to return: after having told all we could to Peterkin about the Diamond Cave under Spouting Cliff, as we named the locality, we were wending our way rapidly homewards, when a grunt and a squeal were borne down by the land-breeze to our ears.

'That's the ticket!' was Peterkin's remarkable exclamation, as he started convulsively, and levelled his spear.

'Hist!' cried Jack; 'these are your friends, Peterkin. They must have come over expressly to pay you a friendly visit, for it is the first time we have seen them on this side the island.'

'Come along!' cried Peterkin, hurrying towards the wood, while Jack and I followed, smiling at his impatience.

Another grunt and half a dozen squeals, much louder than before, came down the valley. At this time we were just opposite the small vale which lay between the Valley of the Wreck and Spouting Cliff.

'I say, Peterkin,' cried Jack, in a hoarse whisper.

'Well, what is't?'

'Stay a bit, man. These grunters are just up there on the hillside. If you go and stand with Ralph in the lee of yon cliff, I'll cut round behind and drive them through the gorge, so that you'll have a better chance of picking out a good one. Now, mind you pitch into a fat young pig, Peterkin,' added Jack, as he sprang into the bushes.

'Won't I just!' said Peterkin, licking his lips, as we took our station beside the cliff. 'I feel quite a tender affection for young pigs in my heart. Perhaps it would be more correct to say in my s——

'There they come!' cried I, as a terrific yell from Jack sent the whole herd screaming down the hill. Now Peterkin, being unable to hold back, crept a short way up a very steep grassy mound, in order to get a better view of the hogs before they came up; and just as he raised his head above its summit, two little pigs, which had outrun their companions, rushed over the top. One of these brushed close past Peterkin's ear; the other, unable to arrest its headlong flight, went, as Peterkin himself afterwards expressed it, 'bash' into his arms with a sudden squeal, which was caused more by the force of the blow than the will of the animal, and both of them rolled violently down to the foot of the mound. No sooner was this reached than the little pig recovered its feet, tossed up its tail, and fled shrieking from the spot. But I slung a large stone after it, which, being fortunately well aimed, hit it behind the ear, and felled it to the earth.

'Capital, Ralph! that's your sort!' cried Peterkin, who, to

my surprise and great relief, had risen to his feet apparently
unhurt, though much dishevelled. He rushed frantically
towards the gorge, which the yells of the hogs told us they were
now approaching. I had made up my mind that I would abstain
from killing another, as, if Peterkin should be successful, two
were more than sufficient for our wants at the present time.
Suddenly they all burst forth—two or three little round ones
in advance, and an enormous old sow with a drove of hogs at
her heels.

'Now, Peterkin,' said I, 'there's a nice little fat one; just
spear it.'

But Peterkin did not move; he allowed it to pass unharmed.
I looked at him in surprise, and saw that his lips were compressed and his eyebrows knitted, as if he were about to fight
with some awful enemy.

'What is it?' I inquired, with some trepidation.

Suddenly he levelled his spear, darted forward, and, with
a yell that nearly froze the blood in my veins, stabbed the old
sow to the heart. Nay, so vigorously was it done that the spear
went in at one side and came out at the other!

'Hallo! what's this?' said Jack, as he came up. 'Why,
Peterkin, you must be fond of a tough chop. If you mean to
eat this old hog, she'll try your jaws, I warrant. What possessed
you to stick *her*, Peterkin?'

'Why, the fact is I want a pair of shoes.'

'What have your shoes to do with the old hog?' said I,
smiling.

'My present shoes have certainly nothing to do with her,'
replied Peterkin; 'nevertheless she will have a good deal to
do with my future shoes. The fact is, when I saw you floor
that pig so neatly, Ralph, it struck me that there was little use
in killing another. Then I remembered all at once that I had
long wanted something to make shoes of, and this old grand-
mother seemed so tough that I just made up my mind to stick
her, and you see I've done it!'

We now considered how we were to carry our game home,
for, although the distance was short, the hog was very heavy.
At length we hit on the plan of tying its four feet together, and
passing the spear handle between them. Jack took one end on

his shoulder, I took the other on mine, and Peterkin carried the small pig.

Thus we returned in triumph to our bower, laden, as Peterkin remarked, with the glorious spoils of a noble hunt.

CHAPTER XV

For many days after this Jack applied himself with unremitting assiduity to the construction of our boat, which at length began to look somewhat like one. But those only who have had the thing to do can entertain a right idea of the difficulty involved in such an undertaking, with no other implements than an axe, a bit of hoop-iron, a sail-needle, and a broken pen-knife. But Jack did it. He was of that disposition which will not be conquered. When he believed himself to be acting rightly, he overcame all obstacles.

As this boat was a curiosity in its way, a few words here relative to the manner of its construction may not be amiss.

I have already mentioned the chestnut tree with its wonderful buttresses or planks. This tree, then, furnished us with the chief part of our material. First of all, Jack sought out a limb of a tree of such a form and size as, while it should form the keel, a bend at either end should form the stem and stern posts. Such a piece, however, was not easy to obtain; but at last we procured it, by rooting up a small tree which had a branch growing at the proper angle about ten feet up its stem, with two strong roots growing in such a form as enabled us to make a flat-sterned boat. This placed, Jack procured three branching roots of suitable size, which he fitted to the keel at equal distances, thus forming three strong ribs. Now the squaring and shaping of these, and the cutting of the grooves in the keel, was an easy enough matter, as it was all work for the axe, in the use of which Jack was become wonderfully expert; but it was quite a different affair when he came to nailing the ribs to the keel, for we had no instrument capable of boring a large hole, and no nails to fasten them with. We were, indeed, much perplexed; but Jack devised an instrument that served very well. He took the remainder of our hoop-iron and beat it into the form of a pipe, about as thick as a man's finger. This he did by means of our axe and the old rusty axe we had found at the house of the poor man at the other side of the island. This, when made red-hot, bored slowly through the timbers; and, the better to retain the heat, Jack shut up one end of it and filled it with sand. True, the work was very slowly done; but we had little else to do. Two holes were bored in each timber, about an inch and a half apart, and also down into the keel, but not quite through. Into these were placed stout pegs made of a tree called iron-wood; and, when they were hammered well home, the timbers were as firmly fixed as if they had been nailed with iron. The gunwales, which were very stout, were fixed in a similar manner. But, besides the wooden nails, they were firmly lashed to the stem and stern posts and ribs by means of a species of cordage which we had contrived to make out of the fibrous husk of the cocoa-nut. This husk was very tough, and when a number of the threads were joined together they formed excellent cordage. At first we tied the different lengths together; but this was such a clumsy and awkward compli- cation of knots that we contrived, by careful interlacing of the ends together before twisting, to make good cordage of any size or length we chose. Of course it cost us much time and labour, but Jack kept up our spirits when we grew weary, and so all that we required was at last constructed.

Planks were now cut off the chestnut trees of about an inch thick. These were dressed with the axe—but clumsily, for an axe is ill-adapted for such work. Five of these planks on each side were sufficient; and we formed the boat in a very rounded, barrel-like shape, in order to have as little twisting of the planks as possible, for although we could easily bend them, we could not easily twist them. Having no nails to rivet the planks with, we threw aside the ordinary fashion of boat-building and adopted one of our own. The planks were therefore placed on each other's edges, and sewed together with the tough cordage already mentioned. They were also thus sewed to the stem, the stern, and the keel. Each stitch or tie was six inches apart, and was formed thus:—Three holes were bored in the upper plank and three in the lower—the holes being above each other, that is, in a vertical line. Through these holes the cord was passed, and, when tied, formed a powerful stitch of three ply. Besides this, we placed between the edges of the planks layers of cocoanut fibre, which, as it swelled when wetted, would, we hoped, make out little vessel water-tight. But in order further to secure this end, we collected a large quantity of pitch from the bread-fruit tree, with which, when boiled in our old iron pot, we payed the whole of the inside of the boat, and, while it was yet hot, placed large pieces of cocoa-nut cloth on it, and then gave it another coat above that. Thus the interior was covered with a tough water-tight material; while the exterior, being uncovered and so exposed to the swelling action of the water, was, we hoped, likely to keep the boat quite dry. I may add that our hopes were not disappointed.

While Jack was thus engaged, Peterkin and I sometimes assisted him; but as our assistance was not much required, we more frequently went a-hunting on the extensive mud-flats at the entrance of the long valley which lay nearest to our bower. Here we found large flocks of ducks of various kinds, some of them bearing so much resemblance to the wild-ducks of our own country that I think they must have been the same. On these occasions we took the bow and the sling, with both of which we were often successful, though I must confess I was the least so. Our suppers were thus pleasantly varied, and sometimes we had such a profusion spread out before us that we frequently knew not with which of the dainties to begin.

I must also add that the poor old cat which we had brought home had always a liberal share of our good things, and so well was it looked after, especially by Peterkin, that it recovered much of its former strength, and seemed to improve in sight as well as hearing.

The large flat rock of coral, which stood just in front of the entrance to our bower, was our table. On this rock we had spread out the few articles we possessed the day we were ship-wrecked; and on the same rock during many a day afterwards, we spread out the bountiful supply with which we had been blessed on our Coral Island. Sometimes we sat down at this table to a feast consisting of hot rolls—as Peterkin called the newly baked bread-fruit—a roast pig, roast duck, boiled and roasted yams, cocoa-nuts, taro and sweet potatoes; which we followed up with a dessert of plums, apples, and plantains—the last being a large-sized and delightful fruit which grew on a large shrub or tree not more than twelve feet high, with light-green leaves of enormous length and breadth. These luxurious feasts were usually washed down with cocoa-nut lemonade.

One day, while Peterkin and I were seated beside our table on which dinner was spread, Jack came up from the beach, and, flinging down his axe, exclaimed:

'There, lads, the boat's finished at last! so we've nothing to do now but shape two pair of oars, and then we may put to sea as soon as we like.'

This piece of news threw us into a state of great joy; for although we were aware that the boat had been gradually getting near its completion, it had taken so long that we did not expect it to be quite ready for at least two or three weeks. But Jack had wrought hard and said nothing, in order to surprise us.

'My dear fellow,' cried Peterkin, 'you're a perfect trump. But why did you not tell us it was so nearly ready? Won't we have a jolly sail to-morrow, eh?'

'Don't talk so much, Peterkin,' said Jack; 'and, pray, hand me a bit of that pig.'

'Certainly, my dear,' cried Peterkin, seizing the axe. 'What part will you have? a leg, or a wing, or a piece of the breast—which?'

'A hind leg, if you please,' answered Jack; 'and, pray, be so be so good as to include the tail.'

'With all my heart,' said Peterkin, exchanging the axe for his hoop-iron knife, with which he cut off the desired portion.

'Well, but,' continued Peterkin, 'I was talking of a sail to-morrow. Can't we have one, Jack?'

'No,' replied Jack, 'we can't have a sail, but I hope we shall have a row, as I intend to work hard at the oars this afternoon, and, if we can't get them finished by sunset, we'll light our candle-nuts, and turn them out before we turn into bed.'

'Very good,' said Peterkin, tossing a lump of pork to the cat, who received it with a mew of satisfaction. 'I'll help you, if I can.'

'Afterwards,' continued Jack, 'we will make a sail out of the cocoa-nut cloth, and rig up a mast, and then we shall be able to sail to some of the other islands, and visit our old friends the penguins.'

The prospect of being so soon in a position to extend our observations to the other islands and enjoy a sail over the beautiful sea afforded us much delight, and after dinner we set about making the oars in good earnest. Jack went into the woods and blocked them roughly out with the axe, and I smoothed them down with the knife, while Peterkin remained in the bower spinning, or rather twisting, some strong thick cordage with which to fasten them to the boat.

We worked hard and rapidly, so that when the sun went down Jack and I returned to the bower with four stout oars, which required little to be done to them save a slight degree of polishing with the knife.

After supper we retired to rest and dream of wonderful adventures in our little boat and distant voyages upon the sea.

CHAPTER XVI

It was a bright, clear, beautiful morning when we first launched our little boat and rowed out upon the placid waters of the lagoon. Not a breath of wind ruffled the surface of the deep. Not a cloud spotted the deep blue sky. Not a sound that was discordant broke the stillness of the morning, although there were many sounds, sweet, tiny and melodious, that mingled in the universal harmony of nature.

At first, in the strength of our delight, we rowed hither and thither without aim or object. But after the effervescence of our spirits was abated, we began to look about us and to consider what we should do.

'I vote that we row to the reef,' cried Peterkin.

'And I vote that we visit the islands within the lagoon,' said I.

'And I vote we do both,' cried Jack; 'so pull away, boys.'

As I have already said, we had made four oars, but our boat was so small that only two were necessary. The extra pair were reserved in case any accident should happen to the others. It was therefore only needful that two of us should row, while the third steered, by means of an oar, and relieved the rowers occasionally.

First we landed on one of the small islands and ran all over it, but saw nothing worthy of particular notice. Then we landed on a larger island, on which were growing a few cocoa-nut trees. Not having eaten anything that morning, we gathered a few of the nuts and breakfasted. After this we pulled straight out to sea and landed on the coral reef.

We had now been so long on shore that we had almost for-gotten the appearance of breakers, for there were none within the lagoon; but now, as we stood beside the foam-crested billow of the open sea, all the enthusiasm of the sailor was awakened in our breasts, and as we gazed on the widespread ruin of that single magnificent breaker that burst in thunder at our feet, we forgot the Coral Island behind us.

This huge, ceaseless breaker, to which I have so often alluded, was a much larger and more sublime object than we had at all imagined it to be. It rose many yards above the level of the sea, and could be seen approaching at some distance from the reef. Slowly and majestically it came on, acquiring greater volume and velocity as it advanced, until it assumed the form of a clear watery arch, which sparkled in the bright sun. On it came with resistless and solemn majesty—the upper edge lipped gently over, and it fell with a roar that seemed as though the heart of Ocean were broken in the crash of tumul-tuous water, while the foam-clad coral reef appeared to tremble beneath the mighty shock!

Having satisfied our curiosity and enjoyed ourselves during the whole day, in our little boat, we returned, somewhat wearied, and, withal, rather hungry, to our bower.

'Now,' said Jack, 'as our boat answers so well, we will get a mast and sail made immediately.'

'So we will,' cried Peterkin, as we all assisted to drag the boat above high-water mark; 'we'll light our candle and set about it this very night. Hurrah, my boys, pull away!'

As we dragged our boat, we observed that she grated heavily on her keel, and as the sands were in this place mingled with broken coral rocks, we saw portions of the wood being scraped off.

'Hallo!' cried Jack, on seeing this; 'that won't do. Our keel will be worn off in no time at this rate.

'So it will,' said I, pondering deeply as to how this might be prevented. But I am not of a mechanical turn naturally, so I could conceive no remedy save that of putting a plate of iron on the keel; but as we had no iron, I knew not what was to be done. 'It seems to me, Jack,' I added, 'that it is impossible to prevent the keel being worn off thus.'

'Impossible!' cried Peterkin. 'My dear Ralph, you are mistaken; there is nothing so easy.'

'How?' I inquired, in some surprise.

'Why, by not using the boat at all!' replied Peterkin.

'Hold your impudent tongue, Peterkin,' said Jack, as he shouldered the oars; 'come along with me and I'll give you work to do. In the first place, you will go and collect cocoa-nut fibre, and set to work to make sewing twine with it——'

'Please, captain,' interrupted Peterkin, 'I've got lots of it made already—more than enough, as a little friend of mine used to be in the habit of saying every day after dinner.'

'Very well,' continued Jack; 'then you'll help Ralph to collect cocoa-nut cloth, and cut it into shape, after which we'll make a sail of it. I'll see to getting the mast and the gearing; so let's to work.'

And to work we went right busily, so that in three days from that time we had set up a mast and sail, with the necessary rigging, in our little boat. The sail was not, indeed, very handsome to look at, as it was formed of a number of oblong patches of cloth; but we had sewed it well by means of our sail-needle, so that it was strong, which was the chief point. Jack had also overcome the difficulty about the keel, by pinning it to a false keel. This was a piece of tough wood, of the same length and width as the real keel, and about five inches deep. He made it of this depth because the boat would

be thereby rendered not only much more safe, but more able
to beat against the wind; which, in a sea where the trade-winds
blow so long and so steadily in one direction, was a matter of
great importance. The piece of wood was pegged very firmly
to the keel; and we now launched our boat with the satisfaction
of knowing that when the false keel should be scraped off we
could easily put on another; whereas, should the real keel have
been scraped away, we could not have renewed it without
taking our boat to pieces, which Peterkin said made his
'marrow quake to think upon'.

The mast and sail answered excellently, and we now sailed
about in the lagoon with great delight, and examined with
much interest the appearance of our island from a distance.
Also, we gazed into the depths of the water, and watched for
hours the gambols of the curious and bright-coloured fish
among the corals and sea-weed. Peterkin also made a fishing-
line, and Jack constructed a number of hooks, some of which
were very good, others remarkably bad. Some of these hooks
were made of iron-wood, which did pretty well, the wood being
extremely hard, and Jack made them very thick and large. Fish
there are not particular. Some of the crooked bones in fish-
heads also answered for this purpose pretty well. But that
which formed our best and most serviceable hook was the brass
finger-ring belonging to Jack. It gave him not a little trouble
to manufacture it. First he cut it with the axe, then twisted it
into the form of a hook. The barb took him several hours to
cut. He did it by means of constant sawing with the broken
pen-knife. As for the point, an hour's rubbing on a piece of
sandstone made an excellent one.

It would be a matter of much time and labour to describe
the appearance of the multitudes of fish that were day after
day drawn into our boat by means of the brass hook.

Sharks did not often appear, but we took care never again
to bathe in deep water without leaving one of our number in
the boat to give us warning, if he should see a shark approaching. As for the whales, they never came into our lagoon, but
we frequently saw them spouting in the deep water beyond the
reef. I shall never forget my surprise the first day I saw one of
these huge monsters close to me. We had been rambling about

on the reef during the morning, and were about to re-embark in our little boat, to return home, when a loud blowing sound caused us to wheel rapidly round. We were just in time to see a shower of spray falling, and the flukes or tail of some monstrous fish disappear in the sea a few hundred yards off. We waited some time to see if he would rise again. As we stood, the sea seemed to open up at our very feet; an immense spout of water was sent with a snort high into the air, and the huge blunt head of a sperm whale rose before us. It was so large that it could easily have taken our little boat, along with ourselves, into its mouth! It plunged slowly back into the sea, like a large ship foundering, and struck the water with its tail so forcibly as to cause a sound like a cannon shot.

We also saw a great number of flying-fish, although we caught none; and we noticed that they never flew out of the water except when followed by their bitter foe the dolphin, from whom they thus endeavoured to escape. But of all the fish that we saw, none surprised us so much as those that we used to find in shallow pools after a shower of rain; and this not on account of their appearance, for they were ordinary-looking and very small, but on account of their having descended in a shower of rain! We could account for them in no other way, because the pools in which we found these fish were quite dry before the shower, and at some distance above high-water mark. Jack, however, suggested a cause which seemed to me very probable. We used often to see waterspouts in the sea. A waterspout is a whirling body of water, which rises from the sea like a sharp-pointed pillar. After rising a good way, it is met by a long tongue, which comes down from the clouds; and when the two have joined, they look something like an hour-glass. The waterspout is then carried by the wind, sometimes gently, sometimes with violence, over the sea, sometimes up into the clouds, and then, bursting, descends in a deluge. This often happens over the land as well as over the sea, and sometimes does much damage, but frequently it passes gently away. Now, Jack thought that the little fish might perhaps have been carried up in a waterspout, and so sent down again in a shower of rain. But we could not be certain as to this point, yet we thought it likely.

During these delightful fishing and boating excursions we caught a good many eels, which we found to be very good to eat. We also found turtles among the coral rocks, and made excellent soup in our iron kettle. Moreover, we discovered many shrimps and prawns, so that we had no lack of variety in our food; and, indeed, we never passed a week without making a new and interesting discovery of some sort or other, either on the land or in the sea.

CHAPTER XVII

One day, not long after our boat was finished, we were sitting on the rocks at Spouting Cliff, and talking of an excursion which we intended to make to Penguin Island the next day.

'You see,' said Peterkin, 'it might be all very well for a stupid fellow like me to remain here and leave the penguins alone, but it would be quite inconsistent with your characters as philosophers to remain any longer in ignorance of the habits and customs of these birds, so the sooner we go the better.'

'Very true,' said I; 'there is nothing I desire so much as to have a closer inspection of them.'

While we were talking, we noticed a dark line, like a low cloud or fog-bank, on the seaward horizon. The day was a fine one, though cloudy, and a gentle breeze was blowing, but the sea was not rougher or the breaker on the reef higher than usual. At first we thought that this looked like a thunder-cloud, and as we had had a good deal of broken weather of late, accompanied by occasional peals of thunder, we supposed that a storm must be approaching. Gradually, however, this line seemed to draw nearer without spreading up over the sky, as would certainly have been the case if it had been a storm-cloud. Still nearer it came, and soon we saw that it was moving swiftly towards the island; but there was no sound till it reached the islands out at sea. As it passed these islands, we observed, with no little anxiety, that a cloud of white foam encircled them, and burst in spray into the air: it was accompanied by a loud roar. This led us to conjecture that the approaching object was an enormous wave of the sea; but we had no idea how large it was till it came near to ourselves. When it approached the outer reef, however, we were awe-struck with its unusual magnitude; and we sprang to our feet, and clambered hastily up to the highest point of the precipice, under an indefinable feeling of fear.

I have said before the the reef opposite Spouting Cliff was very near to the shore, while, just in front of the bower, it was at a considerable distance out to sea. Owing to this formation, the wave reached the reef at the latter point before it struck at the foot of Spouting Cliff. The instant it touched the reef we became aware, for the first time, of its awful magnitude. It burst completely over at all points, with a roar that seemed louder than thunder; and this roar continued for some seconds, while the wave rolled gradually along towards the cliff on which we stood. As its crest reared before us, we felt that we were in great danger, and turned to flee; but we were too late. With a crash that seemed to shake the solid rocks the gigantic billow fell, and instantly the spouting-holes sent up a gush of waterspouts with such force that they shrieked on issuing from their narrow vents. It seemed to us as if the earth had been blown up with water. We were stunned and confused by the shock, and drenched and blinded with spray. At length we all three gained an eminence beyond the reach of the water; but what a scene of devastation met our gaze as we looked along the shore! This enormous wave not only burst over the reef, but continued its way across the lagoon, and fell on the sandy beach of the island with such force that it passed completely over it and dashed into the woods, levelling the smaller trees and bushes in its headlong course.

On seeing this, Jack said he feared our bower must have been swept away, and that the boat, which was on the beach, must have been destroyed. Our hearts sank as we thought of this, and we hastened round through the woods towards our home. On reaching it we found, to our great relief, that the force of the wave had been expended just before reaching the bower; but the entrance to it was almost blocked up by the torn-up bushes and tangled heaps of sea-weed. Having satisfied ourselves as to the bower, we hurried to the spot where the boat had been left; but no boat was there. The spot on which it had stood was vacant, and no sign of it could we see on looking around us.

'It may have been washed up into the woods,' said Jack, hurrying up the beach as he spoke. Still no boat was to be seen, and we were about to give ourselves over to despair, when Peterkin called to Jack and said:

'Jack, my friend, you were once so exceedingly wise as to make me acquainted with the fact that cocoa-nuts grow upon trees; will you now be so good as to inform me what sort of fruit that is growing on the top of yonder bush? for I confess to being ignorant, or, at least, doubtful on the point.'

We looked towards the bush indicated, and there, to our surprise, beheld our little boat snugly nestled among the leaves. We were very much overjoyed at this, for we would have suffered any loss rather than the loss of our boat. We found that the wave had actually borne the boat on its crest from the beach into the woods, and there launched it into the heart of this bush. Had it been tossed against a rock or a tress, it would have been dashed to pieces, whereas it had not received the smallest injury. It was no easy matter, however, to get it out of the bush and down to the sea again. This cost us two days of hard labour to accomplish.

For the benefit of those who interest themselves in the curious natural phenomena of our world, I may mention that a wave of this sort occurs regularly on some of the islands of the Pacific once and sometimes twice in the year. I heard this stated by the missionaries during my career in those seas. They could not tell me whether it visited all of the islands, but I was certainly assured that it occurred periodically in some of them.

After we had got our home put to rights and cleared of the *débris* of the inundation, we again turned our thoughts to paying the penguins a visit. The boat was overhauled and a few repairs done. Then we prepared a supply of provisions, for we intended to be absent at least a night or two. This took us some time to do, for while Jack was busy with the boat, Peterkin was sent into the woods to spear a hog or two, and had to search long, sometimes, to find them. Peterkin was usually sent on this errand when we wanted a pork chop (which was not seldom), because he was so active and could run so wonderfully fast that he found no difficulty in overtaking the hogs; but being dreadfully reckless, he almost invariably tumbled over stumps and stones in the course of his wild chase, and seldom returned home without having knocked the skin off his shins. Once, indeed, a more serious accident happened to him. He had been out all morning alone, and did not return at the usual time to dinner. We wondered at this, for Peterkin was always very punctual at the dinner-hour. As supper-time drew near we began to be anxious about him, and at length went out to search in the woods. For a long time we sought in vain, but a little before dark we came upon the tracks of the hogs, which we followed up until we came to the brow of a rather steep bank or precipice. Looking over this we beheld Peterkin lying in a state of insensibility at the foot, with his cheek resting on the snout of a little pig, which was pinned to the earth by the spear. We were dreadfully alarmed and hastened to bathe his forehead with water, and soon had the satisfaction of seeing him revive. After we had carried him home he related to us how the thing has happened.

'You must know,' said he, 'I walked about all the forenoon, till I was as tired as an old donkey, without seeing a single grunter, not so much as a track of one; but as I was determined not to return empty-handed, I resolved to go without my dinner, and——'

'What!' exclaimed Jack, 'did you *really* resolve to do that?'

'Now, Jack, hold your tongue,' returned Peterkin. 'I say that I resolved to forego my dinner and to push to the head of the small valley, where I felt pretty sure of discovering the hogs. I soon found that I was on the right scent, for I had scarcely walked half a mile in the direction of the small plum-tree we found there the other day, when I heard a squeak. "Ho ho," said I, "there you go, my boys;" and I hurried up the glen. I soon started them, and singling out a fat pig, ran tilt at him. In a few seconds I was up with him, and stuck my spear right through his dumpy body. Just as I did so, I saw that we were on the edge of a precipice. I had been running at such a pace that I could not stop, so the pig and I gave a howl in concert and went plunging over together. I remembered nothing more after that, till I came to my senses and found you bathing my temples, and Ralph wringing his hands over me.'

But although Peterkin was often unfortunate in the way of getting tumbles, he was successful on the present occasion in hunting, and returned before evening with three very nice little hogs. I also was successful in my visit to the mud-flats, where I killed several ducks. So that, when we launched and loaded our boat at sunrise the following morning, we found our store of provisions to be more than sufficient. Part had been cooked the night before, and on taking note of the different items, we found the account to stand thus:—

10 Bread-fruits (two baked, eight unbaked).
20 Yams (six roasted, the rest raw).
 6 Taro-roots.
50 Fine large plums.
 6 Cocoa-nuts, ripe.
 6 Ditto green (for drinking).
 4 Large ducks and two small ones, raw.
 3 Cold roast pigs, with stuffing.

I may here remark that the stuffing had been devised by Peterkin specially for the occasion. He kept the manner of its compounding a profound secret, so I cannot tell what it was; but I can say, with much confidence, that we found it to be atrociously bad, and, after the first tasting, scraped it carefully out and threw it overboard.

It was a very calm sunny morning when we launched the boat, rowed over the lagoon towards the outlet in the reef, and passed between the two green islets that guard the entrance. We experienced some difficulty and no little danger in passing the surf of the breaker, and shipped a good deal of water in the attempt; but, once past the billow, we found ourselves floating placidly on the long oily swell that rose and fell slowly as it rolled over the wide ocean.

Penguin Island lay on the other side of our own island, at about a mile beyond the outer reef, and we calculated that it must be at least twenty miles distant by the way we should have to go. We might, indeed, have shortened the way by coasting round our island inside of the lagoon, and going out at the passage in the reef nearly opposite to Penguin Island; but we preferred to go by the open sea—first, because it was more adventurous, and, secondly, because we should have the pleasure of again feeling the motion of the deep sea.

'I wish we had a breeze,' said Jack.

'So do I,' cried Peterkin, resting on his oar and wiping his heated brow; 'pulling is hard work.'

'But, I say,' remarked Jack, 'it seems that my wish is going to be granted, for here comes a breeze. Ship your oar, Peterkin. Up with the mast, Ralph; I'll see to the sail. Mind your helm; look out for squalls!'

This last speech was caused by the sudden appearance of a dark-blue line on the horizon, which, in an incredibly short space of time, swept down on us, lashing up the sea in white foam as it went. We presented the stern of the boat to its first violence, and, in a few seconds, it moderated into a steady breeze, to which we spread our sail and flew merrily over the waves. Although the breeze died away soon afterwards, it had been so stiff while it lasted that we were carried over the greater part of our way before it fell calm again; so that, when the flapping of the sail against the mast told us that it was time to resume the oars, we were not much more than a mile from Penguin Island.

'There go the soldiers!' cried Peterkin, as we came in sight of it; 'how spruce their white trousers look this morning! I wonder if they will receive us kindly. D'you think they are hospitable, Jack?'

'Don't talk, Peterkin, but pull away and you shall see.'

As we drew near to the island we were much amused by the manœuvres and appearance of these strange birds. They seemed to be of different species, for some had crests on their heads while others had none, and while some were about the size of a goose others appeared nearly as large as a swan. We also saw a huge albatross soaring above the heads of the penguins. It was followed and surrounded by numerous flocks of sea-gulls. Having approached to within a few yards of the

island, which was a low rock with no other vegetation on it
than a few bushes, we lay on our oars and gazed at the birds
with surprise and pleasure, they returning our gaze with
interest. We now saw that their soldier-like appearance was
owing to the stiff, erect manner in which they sat on their short
legs—'bolt-upright', as Peterkin expressed it. They had black
heads, long sharp beaks, white breasts, and bluish backs. Their
wings were so short they looked more like the fins of a fish,
and, indeed, we soon saw that they used them for the purpose
of swimming under water. There were no quills on these wings,
but a sort of scaly feathers, which also thickly covered their
bodies. Their legs were short, and placed so far back that the
birds, while on land, were obliged to stand quite upright in
order to keep their balance; but in the water they floated like
other water-fowl. At first we were so stunned with the clamour
which they and other sea-birds kept up, that we knew not
which way to look—for they covered the rocks in thousands;
but, as we continued to gaze, we observed several quad-
rupeds (as we thought) walking in the midst of the penguins.

'Pull in a bit,' cried Peterkin, 'and let's see what these
are. They must be fond of noisy company, to consort with such
creatures.'

To our surprise we found that these were no other than
penguins which had gone down on all-fours, and were crawl-
ing among the bushes on their feet and wings, just like quadru-
peds. Suddenly one big old bird, that had been sitting on a
point very near to us, became alarmed, and scuttling down the
rocks, plumped or fell, rather than ran, into the sea. It dived
in a moment, and, a few seconds afterwards, came out of the
water far ahead, with such a spring, and such a dive back into
the sea again, that we could scarcely believe it was not a fish
that had leaped in sport.

'That beats everything,' said Peterkin, rubbing his nose,
and screwing up his face with an expression of exasperated
amazement. 'I've heard of a thing being neither fish, flesh,
nor fowl, but I never did expect to live to see a brute that was
all three together—at once—in one! But look there!' he continued, pointing to the shore—'look there! there's no end to it.
What *has* that brute got under its tail?'

We turned to look in the direction pointed out, and there saw a penguin walking slowly and very sedately along the shore with an egg under its tail. There were several others, we observed, burdened in the same way; and we found afterwards that these were a species of penguins that always carried their eggs so. Indeed, they had a most convenient cavity for the purpose, just between the tail and the legs. We were very much impressed with the regularity and order of this colony. The island seemed to be apportioned out into squares, of which each penguin possessed one, and sat in stiff solemnity in the middle of it, or took a slow march up and down the spaces between. Some were hatching their eggs, but others were feeding their young ones in a manner that caused us to laugh not a little. The mother stood on a mound or raised rock, while the young one stood patiently below her on the ground. Suddenly the mother raised her head and uttered a series of the most discordant cackling sounds.

'She's going to choke,' cried Peterkin.

But this was not the case, although, I confess, she looked like it. In a few seconds she put down her head and opened her mouth, into which the young one thrust its beak and seemed to suck something from her throat. Then the cackling was renewed, the sucking continued, and so the operation of feeding was carried on till the young one was satisfied; but what she fed her little one with we could not tell.

'Now, just look yonder!' said Peterkin, in an excited tone. 'That rascally old lady penguin has just pitched her young one into the sea, and there's another about to follow her example.'

We looked to where Peterkin pointed, and, on the top of a steep rock close to the edge of the sea, saw an old penguin endeavouring to entice her young one into the water; but the young one seemed unwilling to go, and, notwithstanding the enticements of its mother, moved very slowly towards her. At last she went gently behind the young bird and pushed it a little towards the water, but with great tenderness, as much as to say, 'Don't be afraid, darling; I won't hurt you, my pet!' but no sooner did she get it to the edge of the rock, where it stood looking pensively down at the sea, than she gave it a sudden and violent push, sending it headlong down the slope into the water, where its mother left it to scramble ashore as it best could. We observed many of them employed in this way, and came to the conclusion that it was the way in which old penguins teach their children to swim.

Scarcely had we finished making our remarks on this, when we were startled by about a dozen of the old birds hopping in the most clumsy and ludicrous manner towards the sea. The beach here was a sloping rock, and when they came to it some of them succeeded in hopping down in safety, but others lost their balance, and rolled and scrambled down the slope in the most helpless manner. The instant they reached the water, however, they seemed to be in their proper element. They dived and bounded out of it and into it again with the utmost agility; and so, diving and bounding and sputtering—for they could not fly—they went rapidly out to sea.

On seeing this, Peterkin turned with a grave face to us and said, 'It's my opinion that these birds are all stark, staring mad, and that this is an enchanted island. I therefore propose that we should either put about ship and fly in terror from the spot, or land valorously on the island, and sell our lives as dearly as we can.'

'I vote for landing; so pull in, lads,' said Jack, giving a stroke with his oar that made the boat spin. In a few seconds we ran the boat into a little creek, where we made her fast to a projecting piece of coral, and running up the beach, entered the ranks of the penguins armed with our cudgels and our spear. We were greatly surprised to find that, instead of attacking us or showing signs of fear at our approach, these curious birds did not move from their places until we laid hands on them, and merely turned their eyes on us in stupid wonder as we passed.

We spent fully three hours on this island in watching the habits of these birds, and when we finally left them, we all three concluded that they were the most wonderful creatures we had ever seen; and further, we thought it probable that they were the most wonderful creatures in the world!

CHAPTER XVIII

It was evening before we left the island of the penguins. As we had made up our minds to encamp for the night on a small island, whereon grew a few cocoa-nut trees, which was about two miles off, we lay to our oars with some energy. But a danger was in store for us which we had not anticipated. The wind, which had carried us so quickly to Penguin Island, freshened as evening drew on to a stiff breeze, and before we had made half the distance to the small island, it became a regular gale. Although it was not so directly against us as to prevent our rowing in the course we wished to go, yet it checked us very much; and although the force of the sea was somewhat broken by the island, the waves soon began to rise, and to roll their broken crests against our small craft, so that she began to take in water, and we had much ado to keep ourselves afloat. At last the wind and sea together became so violent that we found it impossible to make the island, so Jack suddenly put the head of the boat round and ordered Peterkin and me to hoist a corner of the sail, intending to run back to Penguin Island.

'We shall at least have the shelter of the bushes,' he said, as the boat flew before the wind, 'and the penguins will keep us company.'

As Jack spoke, the wind suddenly shifted and blew so much against us that we were forced to hoist more of the sail in order to beat up for the island, being by this change thrown much to leeward of it. What made matters worse was, that the gale came in squalls, so that we were more than once nearly upset.

'Stand by, both of you,' cried Jack, in a quick, earnest tone; 'be ready to douse the sail. I very much fear we won't make the island after all.'

Peterkin and I were so much in the habit of trusting everything to Jack that we had fallen into the way of not considering things, especially such things as were under Jack's care. We had, therefore, never doubted for a moment that all was going well, so that it was with no little anxiety that we heard him make the above remark. However, we had no time for question or surmise, for at the moment he spoke a heavy squall was bearing down upon us, and as we were then flying with our lee gunwale dipping occasionally under the waves, it was evident that we should have to lower our sail altogether. In a few seconds the squall struck the boat, but Peterkin and I had the sail down in a moment. When it was past we were more than half full of water. This I soon baled out, while Peterkin again hoisted a corner of the sail; but the evil which Jack had feared came upon us. We found it quite impossible to make Penguin Island. The gale carried us quickly past it towards the open sea, and the terrible truth flashed upon us that we should be swept out and left to perish miserbaly in a small boat in the midst of the wide ocean.

This idea was forced very strongly upon us because we saw nothing in the direction from which the wind was blowing us save the raging billows of the sea; and, indeed, we trembled as we gazed around us, for we were now beyond the shelter of the islands, and it seemed as though any of the huge billows, which curled over in masses of foam, might swallow us up in a moment. The water, also, began to wash in over our sides, and I had to keep constantly bailing, for Jack could not quit the helm nor Peterkin the sail for an instant. In the midst of this distress Jack uttered an exclamation of hope, and pointed towards a low island or rock which lay directly ahead.

As we neared this rock we observed that it was nothing more than the summit of one of the coral formations, which rose only a few feet above the level of the water, and was, in stormy weather, all but invisible. Over this island the waves were breaking in the utmost fury, and our hearts sank within us as we saw that there was not a spot where we could thrust our little boat without it being dashed to pieces.

'Show a little bit more sail,' cried Jack, as we swept past the weather side of the rock with fearful speed.

'Ay, ay,' answered Peterkin, hoisting about a foot more of our sail.

Little though the addition was, it caused the boat to lie over and creak so loudly, as we cleft the foaming waves, that I expected to be upset every instant; and I blamed Jack in my heart for his rashness. But I did him injustice, for although during two seconds the water rushed in-board in a torrent, he succeeded in steering us sharply round to the leeward side of the rock, where the water was comparatively calm.

'Out your oars now, lads! that's well done. Give way!' We obeyed instantly. The oars splashed into the waves together. One good hearty pull, and we were floating in a comparatively calm creek that was so narrow as to be barely able to admit our boat. Here we were in perfect safety, and as we leaped on shore and fastened our cable to the rocks, I thanked God in my heart for our deliverance from so great danger. But although I have said we were now in safety, I suspect that few of my readers would have envied our position. It is true we had no lack of food but we were drenched to the skin; the sea was foaming round us and the spray flying over our heads, so that we were completely enveloped, as it were, in water; the spot on which we had landed was not more than twelve yards in diameter, and from this spot we could not move without the risk of being swept away by the storm. At the upper end of the creek was a small cave in the rock, which sheltered us from the fury of the winds and waves; and as the rock extended in a sort of ledge over our heads, it prevented the spray from falling upon us.

'Now, boys,' cried Jack, 'bestir yourselves, and let's make ourselves comfortable. Toss out our provisions, Peterkin; and here, Ralph, lend a hand to haul up the boat. Look sharp.'

'Ay, ay, captain,' we cried, as we hastened to obey, much cheered by the hearty manner of our comrade.

Fortunately the cave, although not very deep, was quite dry, so that we succeeded in making ourselves much more comfortable than could have been expected. We landed our provisions, wrung the water out of our garments, spread our sail below us for a carpet, and after having eaten a hearty meal, began to feel quite cheerful. But as night drew on our spirits sank again, for with the daylight all evidence of our security vanished away. We could no longer see the firm rock on which we lay, while we were stunned with the violence of the tempest that raged around us. The night grew pitchy dark as it advanced, so that we could not see our hands when we held them up,

4   (H 840)

before our eyes, and the storm at last became so terrible that it was difficult to make our voices audible. A slight variation of the wind, as we supposed, caused a few drops of spray ever and anon to blow into our faces; and the eddy of the sea, in its mad boiling, washed up into our little creek until it reached our feet and threatened to tear away our boat. In order to prevent this latter calamity, we hauled the boat farther up and held the cable in our hands. Occasional flashes of lightning shone with a ghastly glare through the watery curtains around us, and lent additional horror to the scene. Yet we longed for those dismal flashes, for they were less appalling then the thick blackness that succeeded them. Crashing peals of thunder seemed to tear the skies in twain, and fell upon our ears through the wild yelling of the hurricane as if it had been but a gentle summer breeze; while the billows burst upon the weather side of the island until we fancied that the rock was giving way, and in our agony we clung to the bare ground, expecting every moment to be whirled away and whelmed in the black howling sea.

For three days and three nights we remained on this rock, while the storm continued to rage with unabated fury. On the morning of the fourth day it suddenly ceased, and the wind fell altogether; but the waves still ran so high that we did not dare to put off in our boat. During the greater part of this period we scarcely slept above a few minutes at a time, but on the third night we slept soundly, and awoke early on the fourth morning to find the sea very much down, and the sun shining brightly again in the clear blue sky.

It was with light hearts that we launched forth once more in our little boat and steered away for our island home, which, we were overjoyed to find, was quite visible on the horizon, for we had feared that we had been blown out of sight of it altogether. As it was a dead calm, we had to row during the greater part of the day; but towards the afternoon a fair breeze sprang up, which enabled us to hoist our sail. We soon passed Penguin Island and the other island which we had failed to reach on the day the storm commenced; but as we had still enough of provisions, and were anxious to get home, we did not land.

Although the breeze was pretty fresh for several hours, we

did not reach the outer reef of our island till nightfall, and before we had sailed more than a hundred yards into the lagoon it was late, and the moon and stars were shining brightly. So glad were we to be safe back again on our beloved island, that we scarcely took time to drag the boat a short way up the beach, and then ran up to see that all was right at the bower. On reaching it we found everything just as it had been left, and the poor black cat curled up, sound asleep, on the coral table in front of our humble dwelling.

CHAPTER XIX

For many months after this we continued to live on our island in uninterrupted harmony and happiness. I am certain that none of us wished to be delivered from our captivity, for we were extremely happy, and Peterkin used to say that as we were very young we should not feel the loss of a year or two. Peterkin, as I have said before, was fourteen years of age, Jack eighteen and I fifteen. But Jack was very tall, strong, and manly for his age, and might easily have been mistaken for twenty.

We employed ourselves very busily during this time in making various garments of cocoa-nut cloth, as those with which we had landed were beginning to be very ragged. Peterkin also succeeded in making excellent shoes out of the skin of the old hog, in the following manner:—He first cut a piece of the hide, of an oblong form, a few inches longer than his foot. This he soaked in water, and while it was wet he sewed up one end of it, so as to form a rough imitation of that part of the heel of a shoe where the seam is. This done, he bored a row of holes all round the edge of the piece of skin, through which a tough line was passed. Into the sewed-up part of this shoe he thrust his heel, then drawing the string tight, the edges rose up and overlapped his foot all round. It is true there were a great many ill-looking puckers in these shoes, but we found them very serviceable notwithstanding, and Jack came at last to prefer them to his long boots. We also made various other useful articles, which added to our comfort, and once or twice spoke of building us a house; but we had so great an affection for the bower, and withal found it so serviceable, that we determined not to leave it, nor to attempt the building of a house, which in such a climate might turn out to be rather disagreeable than useful.

We often examined the pistol that we had found in the house on the other side of the island, and Peterkin wished that we had powder and shot, as it would render pig-killing much easier; but, after all, we had become so expert in the use of our sling and bow and spear, that we were independent of more deadly weapons.

Now, while we were engaged with these occupations and amusements, an event occurred one day which was as unexpected as it was alarming and horrible.

Jack and I were sitting, as we were often wont to do, on the rocks at Spouting Cliff, and Peterkin was wringing the water from his garments, having recently fallen by accident into the sea—a thing he was constantly doing—when our attention was suddenly arrested by two objects on the horizon.

'What are yon, think you?' I said, addressing Jack.

'I can't imagine,' answered he. 'I've noticed them for some time, and fancied they were black sea-gulls, but the more I look at them the more I feel convinced they are much larger than gulls.'

'They seem to be coming towards us,' said I.

'Hallo! what's wrong?' inquired Peterkin, coming up.

'Look there,' said Jack.

'Whales!' cried Peterkin, shading his eyes with his hand 'No—eh—*can* they be boats, Jack?'

Our hearts beat with excitement at the very thought of seeing human faces again.

'I think you are about right, Peterkin. But they seem to me to move strangely for boats,' said Jack, in a low tone, as if he were talking to himself.

At last he sprang to his feet. 'They are canoes, Ralph! whether war-canoes or not I cannot tell; but this I know, that most of the natives of the South Sea Islands are cannibals, and have little respect for strangers. We must hide if they land here.'

'How unfortunate,' said I, as we gained the shelter of the bushes, 'that we have forgotten our arms!'

'It does not matter,' said Jack; 'here are clubs enough and to spare.' As he spoke he laid his hand on a bundle of stout poles of various sizes, which Peterkin's ever-busy hands had formed during our frequent visits to the cliff, for no other purpose, apparently, than that of having something to do.

We each selected a stout club according to our several tastes, and lay down behind a rock, whence we could see the canoes approach, without ourselves being seen.

We now observed that the foremost canoe was being chased by the other, and that it contained a few women and children, as well as men—perhaps forty souls altogether; while the canoe which pursued it contained only men. They seemed to be about the same in number, but were better armed, and had the appearance of being a war-party. Both crews were paddling with all their might, and it seemed as if the pursuers exerted themselves to overtake the fugitives ere they could land. In this, however, they failed. The foremost canoe made for the beach close beneath the rocks behind which we were concealed. Their short paddles flashed like meteors in the water, and sent up a constant shower of spray. The foam curled from the prow, and the eyes of the rowers glistened in their black faces as they strained every muscle of their naked bodies; nor did they relax their efforts till the canoe struck the beach with a violent shock; then with a shout of defiance the whole party sprang to the shore. Three women, two of whom carried infants in their arms, rushed into the woods; and the men crowded to the water's edge, with stones in their hands, spears levelled, and clubs brandished, to resist the landing of their enemies.

As the pursuers neared the shore, no sign of fear or hesitation was noticeable. On they came like a wild charger— received but recked not of a shower of stones. The canoe struck, and with a yell the crew leaped into the water, and drove their enemies up the beach.

The battle that immediately ensued was frightful to behold. Most of the men wielded clubs of enormous size and curious shapes, with which they dashed out each other's brains. As they were almost entirely naked, and had to bound, stoop, leap, and run in their terrible hand-to-hand encounters, they looked more like demons than human beings. I felt my heart grow sick at the sight of this bloody battle, and would fain have turned away, but a sort of fascination seemed to hold me with my eyes upon the combatants. I observed that the attacking party was led by a most extraordinary being, who, from his size and peculiarity, I concluded was a chief. His hair was frizzed out to an enormous extent, so that it resembled a large turban. It was dyed a light-yellow hue. He was tattooed from head to foot; and his face, besides being tattooed, was besmeared with red paint, and streaked with white. Altogether, with his yellow turban-like hair, his Herculean black frame, his glittering eyes and white teeth, he seemed most terrible. He was very active in the fight, and had already killed four men.

Suddenly the yellow-haired chief was attacked by a man quite as strong and large as himself. He flourished a heavy club like an eagle's beak at the point. For a second or two these giants eyed each other warily, moving round and round as if to catch each other at a disadvantage; but seeing that nothing was to be gained by this caution, and that the loss of time might turn the tide of battle either way, they apparently made up their minds to attack at the same instant, for, with a wild shout and simultaneous spring, they swung their heavy clubs, which met with a loud report. Suddenly the yellow-haired savage tripped, his enemy sprang forward, the ponderous club was swung, but it did not descend, for at that moment the savage was felled to the ground by a stone from the hand of one who had witnessed his chief's danger. This was the turning-point in the battle. The savages who landed first turned and fled towards the bush, on seeing the fall of their chief. But not one escaped. They were all overtaken and felled to the earth. I saw, however, that they were not all killed. Indeed, their enemies, now that they were conquered, seemed anxious to take them alive; and they succeeded in securing fifteen, whom they bound hand and foot with cords, and laid them among the bushes.

Out of the forty blacks that composed the attacking party, only twenty-eight remained alive, two of whom were sent into the bush to hunt for the women and children.

Jack and Peterkin and I now looked at each other, and whispered our fears that the savages might clamber up the rocks to search for fresh water, and discover our place of concealment; but we were so much interested in watching their movements that we agreed to remain where we were—and, indeed, we could not easily have risen without being seen. One of the savages now went up to the wood, and returned with a bundle of firewood, and set fire to it by the very same means used by Jack the time we made our first fire—namely, with the bow and drill. When the fire was kindled, two of the party went again to the woods and returned with one of the bound men. A dreadful thought flashed upon me that they were going to burn their enemies. I gasped for breath, and seizing my club, endeavoured to spring to my feet; but Jack's powerful arm pinned me to the earth. Next moment one of the savages raised his club and broke the wretched creature's skull. He must have died instantly. Scarcely had his limbs ceased to quiver when the monsters cut slices of flesh from his body, and, after roasting them slightly over the fire, devoured them.

Suddenly there arose a cry from the woods, and in a few seconds the two savages hastened towards the fire dragging the three women and their two infants along with them. One of those women was much younger than her companions, and we were struck with the gentle expression of her face. She and her companions wore short petticoats and a kind of tippet on their shoulders. Their hair was jet black. While we gazed with interest and some anxiety, the big chief advanced to one of the elder females and laid his hand upon the child. But the mother shrank from him, and clasping the little one to her bosom, uttered a wail of fear. With a savage laugh, the chief tore the child from her arms and tossed it into the sea. A low groan burst from Jack's lips as he witnessed this atrocious act and heard the mother's shriek, as she fell insensible on the sand. The rippling waves rolled the child on the beach, as if they refused to be a party in such a foul murder, and we could observe that the little one still lived.

The young girl was now brought forward, and the chief adderssed her; but although we heard his voice and even the words distinctly, of course we could not understand what he said. The girl made no answer to his fierce questions, and we saw by the way in which he pointed to the fire that he threatened her life.

'Peterkin,' said Jack, in a hoarse whisper, 'have you got your knife?'

'Yes,' replied Peterkin, whose face was pale as death.

'That will do. Listen to me, and do my bidding quick.—Here is the small knife, Ralph.—Fly both of you through the bush, cut the cords that bind the prisoners, and set them free.' Jack sprang up, and seized a heavy but short bludgeon, while his strong frame trembled with emotion, and large drops rolled down his forehead.

At this moment the man who had butchered the savage a few minutes before advanced towards the girl with his heavy club. Jack uttered a yell that rang like a death-shriek among the rocks. With one bound he leaped down a precipice full fifteen feet high, and before the savages had recovered from their surprise, was in the midst of them; while Peterkin and I dashed through the bushes towards the prisoners. With one blow of his staff Jack felled the man with the club, then turning round with a look of fury, he rushed upon the big chief of the yellow hair. Had the blow which Jack aimed at his head taken effect, the huge savage would have needed no second stroke; but he was agile as a cat, and avoided it by springing to one side, while, at the same time, he swung his ponderous club at the head of his foe. It was now Jack's turn to leap aside, and well was it for him that the first outburst of his blind fury was over, else he had become an easy prey to his antagonist; but Jack was cool now. He darted his blows rapidly and well, and the superiority of his light weapon was strikingly proved in this combat; for while he could easily evade the blows of the chief's heavy club, the chief could not so easily evade those of his light one. Nevertheless, so quick was he, and so frightfully did he fling about the mighty weapon, that although Jack struck him almost every blow, the strokes had to be delivered so quickly that they wanted force to be effectual.

It was lucky for Jack that the other savages considered the success of their chief in this encounter to be so certain that they refrained from interfering. Had they doubted it, they would have probably ended the matter at once by felling him. But they contented themselves with awaiting the issue.

The force which the chief expended in wielding his club now began to tell. His movements became slower, his breath hissed through his clenched teeth, and the surprised savages drew nearer in order to render assistance. Jack observed this movement. He felt that his fate was sealed, and resolved to cast his life upon the next blow. The chief's club was again about to descend on his head. He might have evaded it easily, but instead of doing so, he suddenly shortened his grasp of his own club, rushed in under the blow, struck his adversary right between the eyes with all his force, and fell to the earth, crushed beneath the senseless body of the chief. A dozen clubs flew high in air, ready to descend on the head of Jack; but they hesitated a moment, for the massive body of the chief completely covered him. That moment saved his life. Ere the savages could tear the chief's body away, seven of their number fell prostrate beneath the clubs of the prisoners whom Peterkin and I had set free, and two others fell under our own hand. We could never have accomplished this had not our enemies been so engrossed with the fight between Jack and the chief that they had failed to observe us until we were upon them. They still outnumbered our party by three; but we were flushed with victory, while they were taken by surprise and dispirited by the fall of their chief. Moreover, they were awe-struck by the sweeping fury of Jack, who seemed to have lost his senses altogether, and had no sooner shaken himself free of the chief's body than he rushed into the midst of them, and in three blows equalized our numbers. Peterkin and I flew to the rescue, the savages followed us, and in less than ten minutes the whole of our opponents were knocked down or made prisoners, bound hand and foot, and extended side by side upon the sea-shore.

CHAPTER XX

After the battle was over, the savages crowded round us and gazed at us in surprise, while they continued to pour upon us a flood of questions, which, being wholly unintelligible, of course we could not answer. However, by way of putting an end to it, Jack took the chief (who had recovered from the effects of his wounds) by the hand and shook it warmly. No sooner did the blacks see that this was meant to express good-will than they shook hands with us all round. After this ceremony was gone through Jack went up to the girl, who had never once moved from the rock where she had been left, but had continued an eager spectator of all that had passed. He made signs to her to follow him, and then, taking the chief by the hand, was about to conduct him to the bower, when his eye fell on the poor infant which had been thrown into the sea and was still lying on the shore. Dropping the chief's hand he hastened towards it, and to his great joy found it to be still alive. We also found that the mother was beginning to recover.

'Here, get out o' the way,' said Jack, pushing us aside, as we stooped over the poor woman and endeavoured to restore her; 'I'll soon bring her round.' So saying, he placed the infant on her bosom and laid its warm cheek on hers. The effect was wonderful. The woman opened her eyes, felt the child, looked at it, and with a cry of joy clasped it in her arms.

'There, that's all right,' said Jack, once more taking the chief by the hand.—'Now, Ralph and Peterkin, make the women and these children follow me to the bower. We'll entertain them as hospitably as we can.'

In a few minutes the savages were all seated on the ground in front of the bower making a hearty meal off a cold roast pig, several ducks, and a variety of cold fish, together with an unlimited supply of cocoa-nuts, bread-fruits, yams, taro, and plums; with all of which they seemed to be quite familiar and perfectly satisfied.

Meanwhile, we three, being thoroughly knocked up with our day's work, took a good draught of cocoa-nut lemonade, and throwing ourselves on our beds fell fast asleep. The savages, it seems, followed our example, and in half an hour the whole camp was asleep.

How long we slept I cannot tell, but this I know, that when we lay down the sun was setting, and when we awoke it was high in the heavens. I awoke Jack, who started up in surprise, being unable at first to comprehend our situation. 'Now, then,' said he, springing up, 'let's see after breakfast.—Hallo, Peterkin, lazy fellow! How long do you mean to lie there?'

By this time the natives outside were all astir, and breakfast in an advanced state of preparation. During the course of it we made sundry attempts to converse with the natives by signs, but without effect. At last we hit upon a plan of discovering their names. Jack pointed to his breast and said 'Jack' very distinctly; then he pointed to Peterkin and to me, repeating our names at the same time. Then he pointed to himself again, and said 'Jack', and laying his finger on the breast of the chief, looked inquiringly into his face. The chief instantly understood him, and said 'Tararo' twice distinctly. Jack repeated it after him, and the chief, nodding his head, approvingly, said 'Chuck'. Then turning towards the youngest of the women, who was seated at the door of the bower, he pointed to her; whereupon the chief said 'Avatea', and pointing towards the sun, raised his finger slowly towards the zenith, where it remained steadily for a minute or two.

'What can that mean, I wonder?' said Jack, looking puzzled.

'Perhaps,' said Peterkin, 'the chief means she is an angel come down to stay here for a while. If so, she's an uncommonly black one!'

We did not feel quite satisfied with this explanation, so Jack went up to her and said 'Avatea'. The woman smiled sadly, and nodded her head, at the same time pointing to her breast and then to the sun, in the same manner as the chief had done. We were puzzled to know what this could signify, but as there was no way of solving our difficulty we were obliged to rest content.

Jack now made signs to the natives to follow him, and taking up his axe, he led them to the place where the battle had been fought. Here we found the prisoners, who had passed the night on the beach, having been totally forgotten by us, as our minds had been full of our guests, and were ultimately overcome by sleep. They did not seem the worse for their exposure, as we judged by the hearty appetite with which they devoured the breakfast that was soon after given to them. Jack then began to dig a hole in the sand, and after working a few seconds, he pointed to it and to the dead bodies that lay exposed on the beach. The natives immediately perceived what he wanted, and running for their paddles, dug a hole in the course of half an hour that was quite large enough to contain all the bodies of the slain. When it was finished they tossed their dead enemies into it with so much indifference that we felt assured they would not have put themselves to this trouble had we not asked them to do so. The body of the yellow-haired chief was the last thrown in.

The next three or four days were spent by the savages in mending their canoe, which had been damaged by the violent shock it had sustained on striking the shore. This canoe was a very curious structure. It was about thirty feet long, and had a high towering stern. The timbers, of which it was partly composed, were fastened much in the same way as those of our little boat were put together; but the part that seemed most curious to us was a sort of outrigger, or long plank, which was attached to the body of the canoe by means of two stout cross-beams. These beams kept the plank parallel with the canoe, but not in contact with it, for it floated in the water with an open space between; thus forming a sort of double canoe. This we found was intended to prevent the upsetting of the canoe, which was so narrow that it could not have maintained an upright position without the outrigger.

When the canoe was ready, we assisted the natives to carry the prisoners into it, and helped them to load it with provisions and fruit. Peterkin also went to the plum-tree for the purpose of making a special onslaught upon the hogs, and killed no less than six of them. These we baked and presented to our friends on the day of their departure. On that day Tararo made a great many energetic signs to us, which, after much consideration, we came to understand were proposals that we should go away with him to his island; but having no desire to do so, we shook our heads very decidedly. However, we consoled him by presenting him with our rusty axe, which we thought we could spare. We also gave him a piece of wood with our names carved on it, and a piece of string to hang it round his neck as an ornament.

An hour later the canoe was out of sight, and we, with an indefinable feeling of sadness creeping round our hearts, were seated in silence beneath the shadow of our bower, meditating on the wonderful events of the last few days.

CHAPTER XXI

One day we were all enjoying ourselves in the Water Garden, preparatory to going on a fishing excursion. Peterkin was sunning himself on the ledge of rock, while we were creeping among the rocks below. Happening to look up, I observed Peterkin cutting the most extraordinary capers and making violent gesticulations for us to come up; so I gave Jack a push and rose immediately.

'A sail! a sail!—Ralph, look; Jack, away on the horizon there, just over the entrance to the lagoon!' cried Peterkin, as we scrambled up the rocks.

'So it is, and a schooner too!' said Jack.

Very soon we perceived that she was making straight for the island, under a steady breeze.

In less than an hour she was close to the reef, where she rounded to, and backed her topsails in order to survey the coast. Seeing this, and fearing that they might not perceive us, we all three waved pieces of cocoa-nut cloth in the air, and soon had the satisfaction of seeing them beginning to lower a boat and bustle about the decks as if they meant to land. Suddenly a flag was run up to the peak, a little cloud of white smoke rose from the schooner's side, and before we could guess their intentions, a cannon-shot came crashing through the bushes, carried away several cocoa-nut trees in its passage, and burst in atoms against the cliff a few yards below the spot on which we stood.

With feelings of terror we now observed that the flag at the schooner's peak was black, with a Death's-head and cross-bones upon it. As we gazed at each other in blank amazement, the word 'pirate' escaped our lips simultaneously.

'What is to be done?' cried Peterkin, as we observed a boat shoot from the vessel's side and make for the entrance of the reef. 'If they take us off the island, it will either be to throw us overboard for sport, or to make pirates of us.'

I did not reply, but looked at Jack, as being our only re-source in this emergency. He stood with folded arms, and his eyes fixed with a grave anxious expression on the ground. 'There is but one hope,' said he, turning with a sad expression of countenance to Peterkin; 'perhaps, after all, we may not have to resort to it. If these villains are anxious to take us, they will soon overrun the whole island. But come, follow me.'

Stopping abruptly in his speech, Jack bounded into the woods, and led us by a circuitous route to Spouting Cliff. Here he halted, and, advancing cautiously to the rocks, glanced over their edge. We were soon by his side, and saw the boat, which was crowded with armed men, just touching the shore. In an in-stant the crew landed, formed line, and rushed up to our bower.

In a few seconds we saw them hurrying back to the boat, one of them swinging the poor cat round his head by the tail. On reaching the water's edge, he tossed it far into the sea, and joined his companions, who appeared to be holding a hasty council.

'You see what we may expect,' said Jack bitterly. 'The man who will wantonly kill a poor brute for sport will think little of murdering a fellow-creature. Now boys, we have but one chance left—the Diamond Cave.'

'The Diamond Cave!' cried Peterkin; 'then my chance is a poor one, for I could not dive into it if all the pirates on the Pacific were at my heels.'

'Now, Peterkin,' said Jack, in a solemn tone, 'you must make up your mind to do it, or we must make up our minds to die in your company.'

'O Jack, cried Peterkin, turning pale, 'leave me; I don't believe they'll think it worth while to kill me. Go, you and Ralph, and dive into the cave.'

'That will not I,' answered Jack quietly, while he picked up a stout cudgel from the ground.—'So now, Ralph, we must prepare to meet these fellows. Their motto is, "No quarter". If we can manage to floor those coming in this direction, we may escape into the woods for a while.'

'There are five of them,' said I; 'we have no chance.'

'Come, then,' cried Peterkin, starting up, and grasping Jack convulsively by the arm, 'let us dive; I will go.'

Those who are not naturally expert in the water know well the feelings of horror that overwhelm them at the bare idea of being held down even for a few seconds; and they will understand the amount of resolution that it required in Peterkin to allow himself to be dragged down to a depth of ten feet, and then, through a narrow tunnel, into an almost pitch-dark cavern. But there was no alternative. The pirates had already caught sight of us, and were now within a short distance of the rocks.

Jack and I seized Peterkin by the arms.

'Now, keep quite still, no struggling,' said Jack, 'or we are lost.'

Peterkin behaved like a hero. He floated passively between us like a log of wood, and we passed the tunnel and rose into the cave in a shorter space of time than I had ever done it before.

Peterkin drew a long, deep breath on reaching the surface, and in a few seconds we were all standing on the ledge of rock in safety. Jack now searched for the tinder and torch which always lay in the cave. He soon found them, and lighting the torch, revealed to Peterkin's wondering gaze the marvels of the place. But we were too wet to waste much time in looking about us. Our first care was to take off our clothes and wring them as dry as we could. This done, we proceeded to examine our larder, for, as Jack truly remarked, there was no knowing how long the pirates might remain on the island.

We now began to make arrangements for spending the night in the cavern. At various periods Jack and I had conveyed cocoa-nuts and other fruits, besides rolls of cocoa-nut cloth, to this submarine cave, partly for amusement, and partly from a feeling that we might possibly be driven one day to take shelter here from the savages. Little did we imagine that the first savages who would drive us into it would be white savages, perhaps our own countrymen. We found the cocoa-nuts in good condition, and the cooked yams, but the bread-fruits were spoiled. We also found the cloth where we had left it, and on opening it out there proved to be sufficient to make a bed; which was important, as the rock was damp. Having collected it all together, we spread out our bed, placed our torch in the midst of us, and ate our supper. It was indeed a strange chamber to feast in; and we could not help remarking on the cold, ghastly appearance of the walls, and the black water at our side, with the thick darkness beyond, and the sullen sound of the drops that fell at long intervals from the roof of the cavern into the still water, and the strong contrast between all this and our bed and supper, which, with our faces, were lit up with the deep red flame of the torch.

At last the faint light that came through the opening died away, warning us that it was night and time for rest. We therefore put out our torch and lay down to sleep.

On awaking, it was some time ere we could collect our faculties so as to remember where we were, and we were in much uncertainty as to whether it was early or late. We saw by the faint light that it was day, but could not guess at the hour; so Jack proposed that he should dive out and reconnoitre.

'No, Jack,' said I; 'do you rest here. You've had enough to do during the last few days. Rest yourself now, and take care of Peterkin, while I go out to see what the pirates are about. I'll be very careful not to expose myself, and I'll bring you word again in a short time.'

'Very well, Ralph,' answered Jack; 'please yourself, but don't be long; and if you'll take my advice you'll go in your clothes, for I would like to have some fresh cocoa-nuts, and climbing trees without clothes is uncomfortable, to say the least of it.'

'The pirates will be sure to keep a sharp look-out,' said Peterkin, 'so pray be careful.'

'No fear,' said I; 'good-bye.'

'Good-bye,' answered my comrades.

And while the words were yet sounding in my ears, I plunged into the water, and in a few seconds found myself in the open air. On rising, I was careful to come up gently and to breathe softly, while I kept close in beside the rocks; but as I observed no one near me, I crept slowly out, and ascended the cliff a step at a time, till I obtained a full view of the shore. No pirates were to be seen—even their boat was gone; but as it was possible they might have hidden themselves, I did not venture too boldly forward. Then it occurred to me to look out at sea, when, to my surprise, I saw the pirate schooner sailing away almost hull down on the horizon! On seeing this I uttered a shout of joy. Then my first impulse was to dive back to tell my companions the good news; but I checked myself, and ran to the top of the cliff, in order to make sure that the vessel I saw was indeed the pirate schooner. I looked long and anxiously at her, and giving vent to a deep sigh of relief, said aloud, 'Yes, there she goes; the villains have been balked of their prey this time at least.'

'Not so sure of that!' said a deep voice at my side, while at the same moment a heavy hand grasped my shoulder, and held it as if in a vice.

CHAPTER XXII

My heart seemed to leap into my throat at the words; and turning round, I beheld a man of immense stature and fierce aspect regarding me with a smile of contempt. He was a white man—that is to say, he was a man of European blood, though his face, from long exposure to the weather, was deeply bronzed. His dress was that of a common seaman, except that he had on a Greek skull-cap, and wore a broad shawl of the richest silk round his waist. In this shawl were placed two pairs of pistols and a heavy cutlass. He wore a beard and moustache, which, like the locks on his head, were short, curly and sprinkled with grey hairs.

'So, youngster,' he said, with a sardonic smile, while I felt his grasp tighten on my shoulder, 'the villains have been balked of their prey, have they? We shall see, we shall see.

Now, you whelp, look yonder.' As he spoke, the pirate uttered a shrill whistle. In a second or two it was answered, and the pirate boat rowed round the point at the Water Garden, and came rapidly towards us. 'Now, go, make a fire on that point; and hark'ee, youngster, if you try to run away, I'll send a quick and sure messenger after you,' and he pointed significantly at his pistols.

I obeyed in silence, and as I happened to have the burning-glass in my pocket, a fire was speedily kindled, and a thick smoke ascended into the air. It had scarcely appeared for two minutes when the boom of a gun rolled over the sea, and looking up, I saw that the schooner was making for the island again. It now flashed across me that this was a ruse on the part of the pirates, and that they had sent their vessel away, knowing that it would lead us to suppose that they had left altogether.

There was a good deal of jesting at the success of their scheme, as the crew ascended the rocks and addressed the man who had captured me by the title of captain. They were a ferocious set of men, with shaggy beards and scowling brows. All of them were armed with cutlasses and pistols, and their costumes were, with trifling variations, similar to that of the captain. As I looked from one to the other, and observed the low, scowling brows that never unbent even when the men laughed, and the mean, rascally expression that sat on each face, I felt that my life hung by a hair.

'But where are the other cubs?' cried one of the men, with an oath that made me shudder. 'I'll swear to it there were three, at least, if not more.'

'You hear what he says, whelp: where are the other dogs?' said the captain.

'If you mean my companions,' said I, in a low voice, 'I won't tell you.'

The pirate captain looked at me in surprise. The drawing a pistol from his belt, he cocked it and said, 'Now, youngster, listen to me. I've no time to waste here. If you don't tell me all you know, I'll blow your brains out! Where are your comrades?'

For an instant I hesitated, not knowing what to do in this extermity. Suddenly a thought occurred to me.

'Villain,' said I, shaking my clenched fist in his face, 'to blow my brains out would make short work of me, and be soon over; death by drowning is as sure, and the agony prolonged: yet, I tell you to your face, if you were to toss me over yonder cliff into the sea, I would not tell you where my companions are, and I dare you to try me!'

The pirate captain grew white with rage as I spoke. 'Say you so?' cried he, uttering a fierce oath.—'Here, lads, take him b' the legs and heave him in—quick!'

The men, who were utterly silenced with surprise at my audacity, advanced and seized me, and as they carried me towards the cliff, I congratulated myself not a little on the success of my scheme, for I knew that once in the water I should be safe, and could rejoin Jack and Peterkin in the cave. But my hopes were suddenly blasted by the captain crying out, 'Hold on, lads, hold on! We'll give him a taste of the thumb-screws before throwing him to the sharks. Away with him into the boat. Look alive! the breeze is freshening.'

The men instantly raised me shoulder high, and hurrying down the rocks, tossed me into the bottom of the boat, where I lay for some time stunned with the violence of my fall.

On recovering sufficiently to raise myself on my elbow, I perceived that we were already outside the coral reef and close alongside the schooner, which was of small size and clipper built. I had only time to observe this much, when I received a severe kick on the side from one of the men, who ordered me, in a rough voice, to jump aboard. Rising hastily, I clambered up the side. In a few minutes the boat was hoisted on deck, the vessel's head put close to the wind, and the Coral Island dropped slowly astern as we beat up against a head sea.

After coming aboard, I remained leaning against the bul-warks close to the gangway. I was surprised to find that there were no guns or carronades of any kind in the vessel, which had more the appearance of a fast-sailing trader than a pirate. But I was struck with the neatness of everything. The brass work of the binnacle and about the tiller, as well as the copper belaying-pins, were as brightly polished as if they had just come from the foundry. The decks were pure white, and smooth. The masts were clean-scraped and varnished, except at the cross-trees and truck, which were painted black. The standing and running rigging was in the most perfect order, and the sails white as snow. In short, everything, from the single narrow red stripe on her low black hull to the trucks on her tapering masts, evinced an amount of care and strict discipline that would have done credit to a ship of the Royal Navy. There was nothing lumbering or unseemly about the vessel, excepting, perhaps, a boat, which lay on the deck with its keel up between the fore and main masts. It seemed disproportionately large for the schooner; but when I saw that the crew amounted to between thirty and forty men, I concluded that this boat was held in reserve in case of any accident compelling the crew to desert the vessel.

I observed that all their arms were sent below; the captain alone retaining his cutlass and a single pistol in the folds of his shawl. Although the tallest and most powerful man in the ship, he did not much excel many of his men in this respect, and the only difference that an ordinary observer would have noticed was a certain degree of straight-forward daring in the bold, ferocious expression of his face, which rendered him less repulsive than his low-browed associates, but did not by any means induce the belief that he was a hero.

But my thoughts soon reverted to the companions whom I had left on shore, and as I turned towards the Coral Island, which was now far away to leeward, I sighed deeply, and the tears rolled slowly down my cheeks as I thought that I might never see them more.

'So you're blubbering, are you, you obstinate whelp?' said the deep voice of the captain, as he came up and gave me a box on the ear that nearly felled me to the deck. 'I don't allow any such weakness aboard o' this ship. So clap a stopper on your eyes, or I'll give you something to cry for.'

I flushed with indignation at this rough and cruel treatment, but felt that giving way to anger would only make matters worse, so I made no reply, but took out my handkerchief and dried my eyes.

'I thought you were made of better stuff,' continued the captain, angrily. 'I'd rather have a mad bull-dog aboard than a water-eyed puppy. But I'll cure you, lad, or introduce you to the sharks before long. Now go below and stay there till I call you.'

As I walked forward to obey, my eye fell on a small keg standing by the side of the main-mast, on which the word *gunpowder* was written in pencil. It immediately flashed across me that, as we were beating up against the wind, anything floating in the sea would be driven on the reef encircling the Coral Island. I also recollected—for thought is more rapid than the lightning—that my old companions had a pistol. Without a moment's hesitation, therefore, I lifted the keg from the deck and tossed it into the sea!

Striding up to me, and uttering fearful imprecations, the captain raised his hand to strike me, while he shouted, 'Boy! whelp! what mean you by that?'

'If you lower your hand,' said I, in a loud voice, while I felt the blood rush to my temples, 'I'll tell you. Until you do so, I'm dumb.'

The captain stepped back and regarded me with a look of amazement.

'Now,' continued I, 'I threw that keg into the sea because the wind and waves will carry it to my friends on the Coral Island, who happen to have a pistol but no powder. I hope that it will reach them soon; and my only regret is that the keg was not a bigger one.'

To my surprise the captain, instead of flying into a rage, smiled, and thrusting his hand into the voluminous shawl that encircled his waist, turned on his heel and walked aft, while I went below.

Here, instead of being rudely handled, as I had expected, the men received me with a shout of laughter, and one of them, patting me on the back, said, 'Well done, lad! you're a brick, and I have no doubt will turn out a rare cove. Bloody Bill there was just such a fellow as you are, and he's now the biggest cut-throat of us all.'

'Take a can of beer, lad,' cried another, 'and wet your whistle after that speech o' your'n to the captain. If any one o' us had made it, youngster, he would have had no whistle to wet by this time.'

'Stop your clapper, Jack,' vociferated a third. 'Give the boy a junk o' meat. Don't you see he's a'most goin' to kick the bucket?'

'And no wonder,' said the first speaker, with an oath, 'after the tumble you gave him into the boat. I guess it would have broke *your* neck if you had got it.'

During the remainder of the afternoon I was left to my own reflections, which were anything but agreeable; for I could not banish from my mind the threat about the thumb-screws, of the nature and use of which I had a vague but terrible conception. I was still meditating on my unhappy fate, when, just after nightfall, one of the watch on deck called down the hatchway:

'Hallo there! one o' you tumble up and light the cabin lamp, and send that boy aft to the captain—sharp!'

'Now then, do you hear, youngster? the captain wants you. Look alive,' said Bloody Bill, raising his huge frame from the locker on which he had been asleep for the last two hours. He sprang up the ladder, and I instantly followed him, and going aft was shown into the cabin by one of the men, who closed the door after me.

A small silver lamp which hung from a beam threw a dim soft light over the cabin, which was a small apartment, and comfortably but plainly furnished. Seated on a camp-stool at the table, and busily engaged in examining a chart of the Pacific, was the captain, who looked up as I entered, and in a quiet voice bade me be seated, while he threw down his pencil, and rising from the table, stretched himself on a sofa at the upper end of the cabin.

'Boy,' said he, looking me full in the face, 'what is your name?'

'Ralph Rover,' I replied.

'Where did you come from, and how came you to be on that island? How many companions had you on it? Answer me, now, and mind you tell no lies.'

'I never tell lies,' said I firmly.

The captain received this reply with a cold, sarcastic smile and bade me answer his questions.

I then told him the history of myself and my companions from the time we sailed till the day of his visit to the island, taking care, however, to make no mention of the Diamond Cave. After I had concluded, he was silent for a few minutes; then looking up, he said, 'Boy, I believe you.'

I was surprised at this remark, for I could not imagine why he should not believe me. However, I made no reply.

'And what,' continued the captain, 'makes you think that this schooner is a pirate?'

'The black flag,' said I, 'showed me what you are; and if any further proof were wanting, I have had it in the brutal treatment I have received at your hands.'

The captain frowned as I spoke, but subduing his anger he continued, 'Boy, you are too bold. I admit that we treated you roughly, but that was because you made us lose time and gave us a good deal of trouble. As to the black flag, that is merely a joke that my fellows play off upon people sometimes in order to frighten them. It is their humour, and does no harm. I am no pirate, boy, but a lawful trader—a rough one, I grant you, but one can't help that in these seas, where there are so many pirates on the water and such murderous black-guards on the land. I carry on a trade in sandal-wood with the Feejee Islands; and if you choose, Ralph, to behave yourself and be a good boy, I'll take you along with me and give you a good share of the profits. You see, I'm in want of an honest boy like you to look after the cabin and keep the log and superintend the traffic on shore sometimes. What say you, Ralph?'

I was much surprised by this explanation, and a good deal relieved to find that the vessel, after all, was not a pirate; but instead of replying, I said, 'If it be as you state, then why did you take me from my island, and why do you not now take me back?'

The captain smiled as he replied, 'I took you off in anger, boy, and I'm sorry for it. I would even now take you back, but we are too far away from it. See, there it is,' he added, laying his finger on he chart, 'and we are now here—fifty miles at least. It would not be fair to my men to put about now, for they have all an interest in the trade.'

I could make no reply to this; so, after a little more conversation, I agreed to become one of the crew, at least until we could reach some civilized island where I might be put ashore. The captain assented to this proposition, and after thanking him for the promise, I left the cabin and went on deck with feelings that ought to have been lighter, but which were, I could not tell why, marvellously heavy and uncomfortable still.

CHAPTER XXIII

Three weeks after the conversation narrated in the last chapter, I was standing on the quarter-deck of the schooner watching the gambols of a shoal of porpoises that swam round us. It was a dead calm. Bloody Bill, as the men called him, was standing at the tiller; but his post for the present was a sine-cure, and he whiled away the time by alternately gazing in dreamy abstraction at the compass in the binnacle, and by walking to the taffrail. In one of these turns he came near to where I was standing, and leaning over the side, looked long and earnestly down into the blue wave.

As he now leaned over the taffrail close beside me, I said to him:

'Bill, why is it that you are so gloomy? Why do you never speak to anyone?'

Bill smiled slightly as he replied, 'Why, I s'pose it's because I hain't got nothin' to say!'

'That's strange,' said I, musingly; 'you look like a man that could think, and such men can usually speak.'

'So they can, youngster,' rejoined Bill, somewhat sternly; 'and I could speak too if I had a mind to, but what's the use o' speakin' here? The men only open their mouths to curse and swear, an' they seem to find it entertainin'; but I don't, so I hold my tongue.'

'Well, Bill, that's true, and I would rather not hear you speak at all than hear you speak like the other men; but I don't swear, Bill, so you might talk to me sometimes, I think. Besides, I'm weary of spending day after day in this way, without a single soul to say a pleasant word to.'

'An' where have you been used to friendly conversation?' said Bill, looking down again into the sea; 'not on that Coral Island, I take it?'

'Yes, indeed,' said I energetically. 'I have spent many of the happiest months in my life on that Coral Island'; and without waiting to be further questioned, I launched out into a glowing account of the happy life that Jack and Peterkin and I had spent together on the island.

'Boy, boy,' said Bill, in a voice so deep that it startled me, 'this is no place for you.'

'That's true,' said I. 'I am of little use on board, and I don't like my comrades; but I can't help it, and at any rate I hope to be free again soon.'

'Free?' said Bill, looking at me in surprise.

'Yes, free,' returned I; 'the captain said he would put me ashore after this trip was over.'

'*This trip*! Hark'ee, boy,' said Bill, lowering his voice, 'what said the captain to you the day you came aboard?'

'He said that he was a trader in sandal-wood, and no pirate, and told me that if I would join him for this trip he would give me a good share of the profits or put me on shore in some civilized island if I chose.'

Bill's brows lowered savagely as he muttered, 'Ay, he said truth when he told you he was a sandal-wood trader, but he lied when——'

'Sail ho!' shouted the look-out at the masthead.

'Where away?' cried Bill, springing to the tiller; while the men, startled by the sudden cry, jumped up and gazed round the horizon.

'On the starboard quarter, hull down, sir,' answered the look-out.

At this moment the captain came on deck, and mounting into the rigging, surveyed the sail through the glass. Then sweeping his eye round the horizon, he gazed steadily at a particular point.

'Take in top-sails,' shouted the captain, swinging himself down on the deck by the main back-stay.

'Take in top-sails,' roared the first mate.

'Ay, ay, sir-r-r,' answered the men, as they sprang into the rigging and went aloft like cats.

Instantly all was bustle on board the hitherto quiet schooner. The top-sails were taken in and stowed, the men stood by the sheets and halyards, and the captain gazed anxiously at the breeze which was now rushing towards us like a sheet of dark blue. In a few seconds it struck us. The schooner trembled as if in surprise at the sudden onset, while she fell away, then bending gracefully to the wind, as though in acknowledgment of her subjection, she cut through the waves with her sharp prow like a dolphin, while Bill directed her course towards the strange sail.

In half an hour we neared her sufficiently to make out that she was a schooner, and we judged her to be a trader. She evidently did not like our appearance, for the instant the breeze reached her she crowded on all sail and showed us her stern. As the breeze had moderated a little, our top-sails were again shaken out, and it soon became evident—despite the proverb, 'A stern chase is a long one'—that we doubled her speed and would overhaul her. When within a mile we hoisted British colours, but receiving no acknowledgment, the captain ordered a shot to be fired across her bows. In a moment, to my surprise, a large portion of the bottom of the boat amidships was removed, and in the hole thus exposed appeared an immense brass gun. It worked on a swivel, and was elevated by means of machinery. It was quickly loaded and fired. The heavy ball struck the water a few yards ahead of the chase, and, ricochetting into the air, plunged into the sea a mile beyond it.

This produced the desired effect. The strange vessel backed her top-sails and hove-to, while we ranged up and lay to about a hundred yards off.

'Lower the boat,' cried the captain.

In a second the boat was lowered and manned by a part of the crew, who were all armed with cutlasses and pistols. As the captain passed me to get into it, he said, 'Jump into the stern-sheets, Ralph; I may want you.' I obeyed, and in ten minutes more we were standing on the stranger's deck. We were all much surprised at the sight that met our eyes. Instead of a crew of such sailors as we were accustomed to see, there were only fifteen blacks standing on the quarter-deck and re-regarding us with looks of undisguised alarm. They were totally unarmed, and most of them unclothed; one or two, however, wore portions of European attire. One had on a pair of duck trousers which were much too large for him, and stuck out in a most ungainly manner. Another wore nothing but the common scanty native garment round the loins and a black beaver hat. But the most ludicrous personage of all, and one who seemed to be chief, was a tall middle-aged man, of a mild, simple expression of countenance, who wore a white cotton shirt, a swallow-tailed coat, and a straw hat, while his black brawny legs were totally uncovered below the knees.

'Where's the commander of this ship?' inquired our captain, stepping up to this individual.

'I is capin,' he answered, taking off his straw hat and making a low bow.

'You!' said our captain, in surprise. 'Where do you come from, and where are you bound? What cargo have you aboard?'

'We is come,' answered the man with the swallow-tail, 'from Aitutaki; we was go for Rarotonga. We is native miss'nary ship; our name is de *Olive Branch*; an' our cargo is two tons cocoa-nuts, seventy pigs, twenty cats, and de Gosp'l.'

This announcement was received by the crew of our vessel with a shout of laughter, which, however, was peremptorily checked by the captain, whose expression instantly changed from one of severity to that of frank urbanity as he advanced towards the missionary and shook him warmly by the hand.

'I am very glad to have fallen in with you,' said he, 'and I wish you much success in your missionary labours. Pray take me to your cabin, as I wish to converse with you privately.'

The missionary immediately took him by the hand, and as he led him away I heard him saying, 'Me most glad to find you trader; we t'ought you be pirate. You very like one 'bout the masts.'

What conversation the captain had with this man I never heard, but he came on deck again in a quarter of an hour, and shaking hands cordially with the missionary, ordered us into our boat and returned to the schooner, which was immediately put before the wind. In a few minutes the *Olive Branch* was left far behind us.

That afternoon, as I was down below at dinner, I heard the men talking about this curious ship.

'I wonder,' said one, 'why our captain looked so sweet on yon swallow-tailed supercargo o' pigs and Gospels. If it had been an ordinary trader, now, he would have taken as many o' the pigs as he required and sent the ship with all on board to the bottom.'

'Why, Dick, you must be new to these seas if you don't know that,' cried another. 'The captain cares as much for the Gospel as you do (an' that's precious little), but he knows, and everybody knows, that the only place among the southern island where a ship can put in and get what she wants in comfort is where the Gospel has been sent to. There are hundreds o' islands, at this blessed moment, where you might as well jump straight into a shark's maw as land without a band o' thirty comrades armed to the teeth to back you.'

'Ay,' said a man with a deep scar over his right eye, 'Dick's new to the work. But if the captain takes us for a cargo o' sandal-wood to the Feejees, he'll get a taste o' these black gentry in their native condition. For my part, I don't know what the Gospel does to them, but I know that when any o' the islands chance to get it, trade goes all smooth and easy.'

'Ralph Rover!' shouted a voice down the hatchway, 'captain wants you aft.',

Springing up the ladder, I hastened to the cabin. On coming again on deck I found Bloody Bill at the helm, and as we were alone together I tried to draw him into conversation. After repeating to him the conversation in the forecastle about the missionaries, I said:

'Tell me, Bill, is this schooner really a trader in sandal-wood?'

'Yes, Ralph, she is; but she's just as really a pirate. The black flag you saw flying at the peak was no deception.'

'Then how can you say she's a trader?' asked I.

'Why, as to that, she trades when she can't take by force; but she takes by force when she can, in preference. Ralph,' he added, lowering his voice, 'if you had seen the bloody deeds that I have witnessed done on these decks, you would not need to ask if we were pirates. But you'll find it out soon enough. As for the missionaries, the captain favours them because they are useful to him. The South Sea islanders are the better of being tamed, and the missionaries are the only men who can do it.'

One day we were becalmed among a group of small islands, most of which appeared to be uninhabited. As we were in want of fresh water, the captain sent the boat ashore to bring off a cask or two. But we were mistaken in thinking there were no natives; for scarcely had we drawn near to the shore when a band of blacks rushed out of the bush and assembled on the beach, brandishing their clubs and spears in a threatening manner. Our men were well armed, but refrained from showing any signs of hostility, and rowed nearer in order to converse with the natives; and I now found that more than one of the crew could speak imperfectly dialects of the language peculiar to the South Sea islanders. When within forty yards of the shore, we ceased rowing, and the first mate stood up to address the multitude; but instead of answering us, they replied with a shower of stones, some of which cut the men severely. Instantly our muskets were levelled, and a volley was about to be fired, when the captain hailed us in a loud voice from the schooner, which lay not more than five or six hundred yards off the shore.

'Don't fire!' he shouted angrily. 'Pull off to the point ahead of you.'

The men looked surprised at this order, and three or four of them hesitated, and seemed disposed to mutiny.

'Don't distress yourselves, lads,' said the mate, while a bitter smile curled his lip. 'Obey orders. The captain's not the man to take an insult tamely. If Long Tom does not speak presently I'll give myself to the sharks.'

The shore was now crowded with a dense mass of savages, amounting probably to five or six hundred. We had not rowed off above a couple of hundred yards when a loud roar thundered over the sea, and the big brass gun sent a withering shower of grape point-blank into the midst of the living mass, through which a wide lane was cut, while a yell, the like of which I could not have imagined, burst from the miserable survivors as they fled to the woods. My blood curdled within me as I witnessed this frightful and wanton slaughter; but I had little time to think, for the captain's deep voice came again over the water towards us: 'Pull ashore, lads, and fill your water-casks.' The men obeyed in silence, and it seemed to me as if even their hard hearts were shocked by the ruthless deed. On gaining the mouth of the rivulet at which we intended to take in water, we found it flowing with blood, for the greater part of those who were slain had been standing on the banks of the stream, a short way above its mouth. No one dared to oppose our landing now, so we carried our casks to a pool above the murdered group, and having filled them, returned on board.

'And this,' thought I, gazing in horror at the captain, who, with a quiet look of indifference, leaned upon the taffrail smoking a cigar and contemplating the fertile green islets as they passed like a lovely picture before our eyes—'this is the man who favours the missionaries because they are useful to him and can tame the savages better than anyone else can do it!'

CHAPTER XXIV

It was many days after the events just narrated here I recovered a little of my wonted spirits. I could not shake off the feeling for a long time that I was in a frightful dream, and the sight of our captain filled me with so much horror that I kept out of his way as much as my duties about the cabin would permit. Fortunately he took so little notice of me that he did not observe my changed feelings towards him, otherwise it might have been the worse for me.

But I was now resolved that I would run away the very first island we should land at, and commit myself to the hospitality of the natives rather than remain an hour longer than I could help in the pirate schooner. I pondered this subject a good deal, and at last made up my mind to communicate my intention to Bloody Bill; for during several talks I had had with him of late, I felt assured that he too would willingly escape if possible. When I told him of my design, he shook his head. 'No, no, Ralph,' said he, 'you must not think of running away here. Among some of the groups of islands you might do so with safety, but if you tried it here you would find that you had jumped out of the fryin'-pan into the fire.'

'How so, Bill?' said I; 'would the natives not receive me?'

'That they would, lad; but they would eat you too.'

'Eat me!' said I, in surprise; 'I thought the South Sea islanders never ate anybody except their enemies.'

"Humph!" ejaculated Bill. 'I s'pose 'twas yer tender-hearted friends in England that put that notion into your head. There's a set o' soft-hearted folk at home that I knows on who don't like to have their feelin's ruffled. I know for certain, and many captains of the British and American navies know as well as me, that the Feejee islanders eat not only their enemies but one another; and they do it not for spite, but for pleasure. It's a *fact* that they prefer human flesh to any other. But they don't like white men's flesh so well as black; they say it makes them sick.'

'Why, Bill,' said I, 'you told me just now that they would eat *me* if they caught me.'

'So I did, and so I think they would. I've only heard some o' them say they don't like white men *so well* as black; but if they was hungry they wouldn't be particular. Anyhow, I'm sure they would kill you. You see, Ralph, I've been a good while in them parts, and I've visited the different groups of islands oftentimes as a trader. And thorough-goin' black-guards some o' them traders are; no better than pirates, I can tell you. One captain that I sailed with was not a chip better than the one we're with now. He was trading with a friendly chief one day, aboard his vessel. The chief had swum off to us with the things for trade tied atop his head, for them chaps are like otters in the water. Well, the chief was hard on the captain, and would not part with some o' his things. When their bargainin' was over they shook hands, and the chief jumped overboard to swim ashore; but before he got forty yards from the ship the captain seized a musket and shot him dead. He then hove up anchor and put to sea, and as we sailed

along shore, he dropped six black fellows with his rifle, re-
markin' that "that would spoil the trade for the next comers"
But, as I was saying', I'm up to the ways o' these fellows. One
o' the laws o' the country is, that every shipwrecked person
who happens to be cast ashore, be he dead or alive, is doomed
to be roasted and eaten.'

I was very much shocked and cast down in my mind at this
terrible account of the natives, and asked Bill what he would
advise me to do. Looking round the deck to make sure that
we were not overheard, he lowered his voice and said, 'There
are two or three ways that we might escape, Ralph, but none
o' them's easy. If the captain would only sail for some o' the
islands near Tahiti, we might run away there well enough,
because the natives are all Christians; an' we find that where-
ever the savages take up with Christianity they always give over
their bloody ways, and are safe to be trusted. However, the
captain always keeps a sharp look-out after us when we get to
these islands, for he half suspects that one or two o' us are tired
of his company. Then we might manage to cut the boat adrift
some fine night when it's our watch on deck, and clear off
before they discovered that we were gone. But we would run
the risk o' bein' caught by the blacks. I wouldn't like to try
that plan. But you and I will think over it, Ralph, and see
what's to be done. In the meantime it's our watch below, so
I'll go and turn in.'

Bill then bade me good-night, and went below. I walked
aft, and leaning over the stern, looked down into the phos-
phorescent waves that gurgled around the rudder, and steamed
out like a flame of blue light in the vessel's wake. My thoughts
were very sad, and I could scarce refrain from tears as I con-
trasted my present wretched positions with the happy, peaceful
time I had spent on the Coral Island with my dear companions.
As I thought upon Jack and Peterkin anxious foreboding
crossed my mind, and I pictured to myself the grief and dismay
with which they would search every nook and corner of the
island, in a vain attempt to discover my dead body; for I felt
assured that if they did not see any sign of the pirate schooner
or boat when they came out of the cave to look for me, they
would never imagine that I had been carried away. I wondered,

too, how Jack would succeed in getting Peterkin out of the cave without my assistance; and I trembled when I thought that Peterkin might lose presence of mind, and begin to kick when he was in the tunnel! These thoughts were suddenly interrupted and put to flight by a bright red blaze which lighted up the horizon to the southward and cast a crimson glow far over the sea. It was accompanied by a low growling sound, as of distant thunder, and at the same time the sky above us became black, while a hot stifling wind blew around us in fitful gusts.

The crew assembled hastily on deck, and most of them were under the belief that a frightful hurricane was pending; but the captain, coming on deck, soon explained the phenomena.

'It's only a volcano,' said he. 'I knew there was one hereabouts, but thought it was extinct.—Up there and furl topgallant-sails; we'll likely have a breeze, and it's well to be ready.'

As he spoke a shower began to fall, which we quickly observed was not rain but fine ashes. As we were many miles distant from the volcano, these must have been carried to us from it by the wind. As the captain had predicted, a stiff breeze soon afterwards sprang up, under the influence of which we speedily left the volcano far behind us; but during the greater part of the night we could see its lurid glare and hear its distant thunder. The shower did not cease to fall for several hours, and we must have sailed under it for nearly forty miles, perhaps farther. When we emerged from the cloud, our decks and rigging were covered with a thick coat of ashes.

Three days afterwards, we found ourselves a few miles to windward of an island of considerable size and luxuriant aspect. Bloody Bill was beside me when it first hove in sight.

'Ha!' he exclaimed, 'I know that island well. They call if Emo.'

'Have you been here before, then?' I inquired.

'Ay, that I have, often, and so has this schooner. 'Tis a famous island for sandal-wood. We have taken many cargoes off it already, and have paid for them, too; for the savages are so numerous that we dared not try to take it by force. But our captain has tried to cheat them so often that they're beginning not to like us overmuch now.'

5

We soon ran inside the barrier coral-reef, and let go our anchor in six fathoms water, just opposite the mouth of a small creek, whose shores were densely covered with mangroves and tall umbrageous trees. The principal village of the natives lay about half a mile from this point. Ordering the boat out, the captain jumped into it, and ordered me to follow him. The men, fifteen in number, were well armed; and the mate was directed to have Long Tom ready for emergencies.

'Give way, lads,' cried the captain.

The oars fell into the water at the word, the boat shot from the schooner's side, and in a few minutes reached the shore. Here, contrary to our expectation, we were met with the utmost cordiality by Romata, the principal chief of the island, who conducted us to his house and gave us mats to sit upon. I observed in passing that the natives, of whom there were two or three thousand, were totally unarmed.

After a short preliminary palaver, a feast of baked pigs and various roots was spread before us; of which we partook sparingly, and then proceeded to business. The captain stated his object in visiting the island, regretted that there had been a slight misunderstanding during the last visit, and hoped that no ill-will was borne by either party, and that a satisfactory trade would be accomplished.

Romata answered that he had forgotten there had been any differences between them, protested that he was delighted to see his friends again, and assured them they should have every assistance in cutting and embarking the wood. The terms were afterwards agreed on, and we rose to depart. All this conversation was afterwards explained to me by Bill, who understood the language pretty well.

Romata accompanied us on board, and explained that a great chief from another island was then on a visit to him, and that he was to be ceremoniously entertained on the following day. After begging to be allowed to introduce him to us, and receiving permission, he sent his canoe ashore to bring him off. At the same time he gave orders to bring on board his two favourites, a cock and a paroquet. While the canoe was gone on this errand, I had time to regard the savage chief attentively. Romata was a man of great size, with massive but beautifully moulded limbs and figure, broad chest, and muscular arms. He wore a black beard and moustache, and his hair was frizzed out to such an extent that it resembled a large turban, in which was stuck a long wooden pin!

In ten minutes the canoe returned, bringing the other chief, who certainly presented a most extraordinary appearance, having painted one half of his face red and the other half yellow, besides ornamenting it with various designs in black! As this chief had never seen a ship before, except, perchance, some of the petty traders that at long intervals visit these remote islands, he was much taken up with the neatness and beauty of all the fittings of the schooner. He was particularly struck with a musket which was shown to him, and asked where the white men got hatchets hard enough to cut the tree of which the barrel was made! While he was thus engaged, his brother chief stood aloof, talking with the captain, and fondling a superb cock and a little blue-headed paroquet, the favourites of which I have before spoken. I observed that all the other natives walked in a crouching posture while in the presence of Romata. Before our guests left us, the captain ordered the brass gun to be uncovered and fired for their gratification; and I have every reason to believe he did so for the purpose of showing our superior power, in case the natives should harbour any evil designs against us.

Next day the crew went ashore to cut sandal-wood, while the captain, with one or two men, remained on board, in order to be ready, if need be, with the brass gun, which was unhoused and conspicuously elevated, with its capacious muzzle directed point-blank at the chief's house. The men were fully armed as usual; and the captain ordered me to go with them, to assist in the work.

As we wound along in single file through the rich fragrant groves of banana, cocoa-nut, bread-fruit, and other trees, I observed that there were many of the plum and banyan trees, with which I had become familiar on the Coral Island. I noticed also large quantities of taro-roots, yams, and sweet potatoes growing in enclosures. On turning into an open glade of the woods, we came abruptly upon a cluster of native houses. They were built chiefly of bamboos, and were thatched with the large thick leaves of the pandanus; but many of them had little more than a sloping roof and three sides with an open front, being the most simple shelter from the weather that could well be imagined. Within these and around them were groups of natives—men, women, and children—who all stood up to gaze at us as we marched along, followed by the party of men whom the chief had sent to escort us. About half a mile inland we arrived at the spot where the sandal-wood grew, and while the men set to work I clambered up an adjoining hill to observe the country.

About midday the chief arrived with several followers, one of whom carried a baked pig on a wooden platter, with yams and potatoes on several plantain leaves, which he presented to the men, who sat down under the shade of a tree to dine. The chief sat down to dine also; but to my surprise, instead of feeding himself was fed by one of his wives.

The next day I had an opportunity of witnessing swimming in the surf.

I suppose it was in honour of their guest that this grand swimming-match was got up, for Romata came and told the captain that they were going to engage in it, and begged him to 'come and see'.

'What sort of amusement is this surf-swimming?' I inquired of Bill, as we walked together to a part of the shore on which several thousands of the natives were assembled.

'It's a very favoutite lark with these 'xtr'or'nary critters,' replied Bill, giving a turn to the quid of tobacco that invariably bulged out his left cheek. 'But there they go!'

As he spoke, several hundreds of the natives, amongst whom we were now standing, uttered a loud yell, rushed down the beach, plunged into the surf, and were carried off by the seething foam of the retreating wave.

At the point where we stood, the encircling coral reef joined the shore, so that the breakers, which a recent stiff breeze had rendered larger than usual, fell in thunder at the feet of the multitudes who lined the beach. For some time the swimmers continued to strike out to sea, breasting over the swell like hundreds of black seals. Then they all turned, and watching an approaching billow, mounted its white crest, and each laying his breast on the short flat board, came rolling towards the shore, careering on the summit of the mighty wave, while they and the onlookers shouted and yelled with excitement. Just as the monster wave curled in solemn majesty to fling its bulky weight upon the beach, most of the swimmers slid back into the trough behind; others slipping off their boards, seized them in their hands, and plunging through the watery waste, swam out to repeat the amusement; but a few, who seemed to me the most reckless, continued their career until they were launched upon the beach, and enveloped in the churning foam and spray. One of these last came in on the crest of the wave most manfully, and landed with a violent bound almost on the spot where Bill and I stood. I saw by his peculiar head-dress that he was the chief whom the tribe entertained as their guest.

At this moment we were startled by the cry of 'Mao! mao! —a shark! a shark!' which was immediately followed by a shriek that rang clear and fearfully loud above the tumult of cries that arose from the savages in the water and on the land. We turned hastily towards the direction whence the cry came, and had just time to observe the glaring eyeballs of one of the swimmers as he tossed his arms in the air. Next instant he was pulled under the waves. A canoe was instantly launched, and the hand of the drowning man was caught, but only half of his body was dragged from the maw of the monster, which followed the canoe until the water became so shallow that it could scarcely swim. The crest of the next billow was tinged with red as it rolled towards the shore.

In most countries of the world this would have made a deep impression on the spectators, but the only effect it had upon these islanders was to make them hurry with all speed out of the sea, least a similar fate should befall some of the others; but so utterly reckless were they of human life, that it did not for a moment suspend the progress of their amusements. It is true the surf-swimming ended for that time somewhat abruptly, but they immediately proceeded with other games. Bill told me that sharks do not often attack the surf-swimmers, being frightened away by the immense numbers of men and boys in the water, and by the shouting and splashing that they make. 'But,' said he, 'such a thing as you have seen just now don't frighten them much. They'll be at it again to-morrow or next day, just as if there wasn't a single shark between Feejee and Nova Zembla.'

After this the natives had a series of wrestling and boxing matches; and being men of great size and muscle, they did a good deal of injury to each other, especially in boxing, in which not only the lower orders but several of the chiefs and priests engaged. Each bout was very quickly terminated, for they did not pretend to a scientific knowledge of the art, and wasted no time in sparring, but hit straight out at each other's heads, and their blows were delivered with great force. Frequently one of the combatants was knocked down with a single blow.

I was struck with the beauty of many of the figures and designs that were tattooed on the persons of the chiefs and principal men. One figure, that seemed to me very elegant, was that of a palm tree tattooed on the back of a man's leg, the roots rising, as it were, from under his heel, the stem ascending the tendon of the ankle, and the graceful head branching out upon the calf. I afterwards learned that this process of tattooing is very painful, and takes long to do, commencing at the age of ten, and being continued at intervals up to the age of thirty. It is done by means of an instrument made of bone, with a number of sharp teeth with which the skin is punctured. Into these punctures a preparation made from the kernel of the candle-nut, mixed with cocoa-nut oil, is rubbed, and the mark thus made is indelible. The operation is performed by a class of men whose profession it is, and they tattoo as much at a time as the person on whom they are operating can bear; which is not much, the pain and inflammation caused by tattooing being very great, sometimes causing death.

CHAPTER XXV

Next day I awoke with a feverish brow and a feeling of deep depression at my heart, and the more I thought on my unhappy fate, the more wretched and miserable did I feel.

I was surrounded on all sides by human beings of the most dreadful character, to whom the shedding of blood was mere pastime. On shore were the natives, whose practices were so horrible that I could not think of them without shuddering. Even Bill, with whom I had, under the strange circumstances of my lot, formed a kind of intimacy, was so fierce in his nature as to have acquired the title of 'Bloody'.

When the captain came on deck, before the hour at which the men usually started for the woods, I begged of him to permit me to remain aboard that day, as I did not feel well; but he looked at me angrily, and ordered me, in a surly tone, to get ready to go on shore as usual. The fact was that the captain had been out of humour for some time past. Romata and he had had some differences, and high words had passed between them, during which the chief had threatened to send a fleet of his war-canoes, with a thousand men, to break up and burn the schooner; whereupon the captain smiled sarcastically, and going up to the chief gazed sternly in his face, while he said, 'I have only to raise my little finger just now, and my big gun will blow your whole village to atoms in five minutes!' Although the chief was a bold man, he quailed before the pirate's glance and threat, and made no reply; but a bad feeling had been raised, and old sores had been opened.

I had, therefore, to go with the wood-cutters that day. Before starting, however, the captain called me into the cabin, and said:

'Here, Ralph. That blackguard Romata is in the dumps, and nothing will mollify him but a gift; so do you go up to his house and give him these whale's teeth, with my compliments. Take with you one of the men who can speak the language.'

I looked at the gift in some surprise, for it consisted of six white whale's teeth, and two of the same dyed bright red, which seemed to me very paltry things. However, I did not dare to hesitate or ask any questions; so gathering them up, I left the cabin, and was soon on my way to the chief's house, accompanied by Bill. On my expressing surprise at the gift, he said:

'They're paltry enough to you or me, Ralph, but they're

considered of great value by them chaps. They're a sort o' cash among them. The red ones are the most prized, one of them bein' equal to twenty o' the white ones. I suppose the only reason for their bein' valuable is that there ain't many of them, and they're hard to be got.'

On arriving at the house we found Romata sitting on a mat, in the midst of a number of large bales of native cloth and other articles which had been brought to him as presents from time to time by inferior chiefs. He received us rather haughtily, but on Bill explaining the nature of our errand he became very condescending, and his eyes glistened with satisfaction when he received the whale's teeth, although he laid them aside with an assumption of kingly indifference.

'Go,' said he, with a wave of the hand—'go tell your captain that he may cut wood to-day, but not to-morrow. He must come ashore; I want to have a palaver with him.'

As we left the house Bill shook his head.

'There's mischief brewin' in that black rascal's head.'

In the course of the evening I overheard part of a conversation between the captain and the first mate, which startled me not a little. They were down in the cabin, and conversed in an undertone; but the skylight being off, I overheard every word that was said.

'I don't half like it,' said the mate. 'It seems to me that we'll only have hard fightin' and no pay.'

'No pay!' repeated the captain, in a voice of suppressed anger. 'Do you call a good cargo all for nothing no pay?'

'Very true,' returned the mate; 'but we've got the cargo aboard. Why not cut your cable and take French leave o' them? What's the use o' tryin' to lick the blackguards when it'll do us no manner o' good?'

'Mate,' said the captain, in a low voice, 'you talk like a fresh-water sailor. I can only attribute this shyness to some strange delusion; for surely' (his voice assumed a slightly sneering tone as he said this), 'surely I am not to suppose that *you* have become soft-hearted! Besides, you are wrong in regard to the cargo being aboard; there's a good quarter of it lying in the woods, and that blackguard chief knows it and won't let me take it off. He defied us to do our worst yesterday.'

'Defied us! did he?' cried the mate, with a bitter laugh. 'Poor contemptible thing!'

'And yet he seems not so contemptible but that you are afraid to attack him.'

'Who said I was afraid?' growled the mate sulkily. 'But, captain, what is it that you intend to do?'

'I intend to muffle the sweeps and row the schooner up to the head of the creek there, from which point we can command the pile of sandal-wood with our gun. Then I shall land with all the men except two, who shall take care of the schooner and be ready with the boat to take us off. We can creep through the woods to the head of the village, where these cannibals are always dancing round, and if the carbines of the men are loaded with a heavy charge of buck-shot, we can drop forty or fifty at the first volley. After that the thing will be easy enough. The savages will take to the mountains in a body, and we shall take what we require, up anchor, and away.'

To this plan the mate at length agreed. As he left the cabin I heard the captain say:

'Give the men an extra glass of grog, and don't forget the buck-shot.'

The reader may conceive the horror with which I heard this murderous conversation. I immediately repeated it to Bill, who seemed much perplexed about it. At length he said:

'I'll tell you what I'll do, Ralph. I'll swim ashore after dark and fix a musket to a tree not far from the place where we'll have to land, and I'll tie a long string to the trigger, so that when our fellows cross it they'll let it off, and so alarm the village in time to prevent an attack, but not in time to prevent us gettin' back to the boat. So, Master Captain,' added Bill, with a smile that for the first time seemed to me to be mingled with good-natured cheerfulness, 'you'll be balked at least for once in your life by Bloody Bill.'

After it grew dark, Bill put this resolve in practice. He slipped over the side with a musket in his left hand, while with his right he swam ashore and entered the woods. He soon returned, having accomplished his purpose, and got on board without being seen.

When the hour of midnight approached, the men were

mustered on deck, the cable was cut and the muffled sweeps got out. These sweeps were immensely large oars, each requiring a couple of men to work it. In a few minutes we entered the mouth of the creek, which was indeed the mouth of a small river, and took about half an hour to ascend, although the spot where we intended to land was not more than six hundred yards from the mouth. There was a slight current against us, and the mangroves which narrowed the creek impeded the rowers in some places. Having reached the spot, which was so darkened by overhanging trees that we could see with difficulty, a small kedge anchor attached to a thin line was let softly down over the stern.

'Now, lads,' whispered the captain, as he walked along the line of men, who were all armed to the teeth, 'don't be in a hurry, aim low, and don't waste your first shots.'

He then pointed to the boat, into which the men crowded in silence. There was no room to row; but oars were not needed, as a slight push against the side of the schooner sent the boat gliding to the shore.

'There's no need of leaving two in the boat,' whispered the mate, as the men stepped out; 'we shall want all our hands. Let Ralph stay.'

The captain assented, and ordered me to stand in readiness, with the boat-hook, to shove ashore at a moment's notice if they should return, or to shove off if any of the savages should happen to approach. He then threw his carbine into the hollow of his arm and glided through the bushes, followed by his men. With a throbbing heart I awaited the result of our plan. I knew the exact locality where the musket was placed, for Bill had described it to me, and I kept my straining eyes fixed upon the spot. But no sound came, and I began to fear that either they had gone in another direction or that Bill had not fixed the string properly. Suddenly I heard a faint click, and observed one or two bright sparks among the bushes. My heart immediately sank within me, for I knew at once that the trigger had indeed been pulled, but that the priming had not caught. The plan, therefore, had utterly failed. A feeling of dread now began to creep over me as I stood in the boat, in that dark, silent spot, awaiting the issue of this murderous expedition.

Suddenly I heard a shot. In a moment a thousand voices raised a yell in the village; again the cry rose on the night air, and was followed by broken shouts as of scattered parties of men bounding into the woods. Then I heard another shout loud and close at hand. It was the voice of the captain cursing the man who had fired the premature shot. Then came the order, 'Forward!' followed by the wild hurrah of our men as they charged the savages. Shots now rang in quick succession, and at last a loud volley startled the echoes of the woods. It was followed by a multitude of wild shrieks, which were immediately drowned in another hurrah from the men; the distance of the sound proving that they were driving their enemies before them towards the sea.

While I was listening intently to these sounds, which were now mingled in confusion, I was startled by the rustling of the leaves not far from me. At first I thought it was a party of savages who had observed the schooner, but I was speedily undeceived by observing a body of natives—apparently several hundreds, as far as I could guess in the uncertain light—bounding through the woods towards the scene of battle. I saw at once that this was a party who had outflanked our men, and would speedily attack them in the rear. And so it turned out; for in a short time the shouts increased tenfold.

At length the tumult of battle ceased, and from the cries of exultation that now arose from the savages, I felt assured that our men had been conquered. I was immediately thrown into dreadful consternation. What was I now to do? To be taken by the savages was too horrible to be thought of; to flee to the mountains was hopeless, as I should soon be discovered; and to take the schooner out of the creek without assistance was impossible. I resolved, however, to make the attempt, as being my only hope, and was on the point of pushing off, when my hand was stayed, and my blood chilled by an appalling shriek, in which I recognized the voice of one of the crew. It was succeeded by a shout from the savages. Then came another and another shriek of agony, making my ears to tingle, as I felt convinced they were murdering the pirate crew. With a bursting heart and my brain whirling as if on fire, I seized the boat-hook to push from shore, when a man sprang from the bushes.

'Stop! Ralph, stop!—there now, push off,' he cried, and bounded into the boat so violently as nearly to upset her. It was Bill's voice! In another moment we were on board—the boat made fast, the line of the anchor cut, and the sweeps run out. At the first stroke of Bill's giant arm the schooner was nearly pulled ashore, for in his haste he forgot that I could scarcely move the unwieldy oar. Springing to the stern, he lashed the rudder in such a position that, while it aided me, it acted against him, and so rendered the force of our strokes nearly equal. The schooner now began to glide quickly down the creek; but before we reached its mouth, a yell from a thousand voices on the bank told that we were discovered. Instantly a number of the savages plunged into the water and swam towards us; but we were making so much way that they could not overtake us. One powerful man, however, succeeded in laying hold of the cut rope that hung from the stern, and clambered quickly upon deck. Bill caught sight of him the instant his head appeared above the taffrail. But he did not cease to row, and did not appear even to notice the savage until he was within a yard of him; then dropping the sweep, he struck him a blow on the forehead with his clenched fist that felled him to the deck. Lifting him up, he hurled him overboard and resumed the oar. But now a greater danger awaited us, for the savages had outrun us on the bank, and were about to plunge into the water ahead of the schooner. If they succeeded in doing so our fate was sealed. For one moment Bill stood irresolute. Then drawing a pistol from his belt, he sprang to the brass gun, held the pan of his pistol over the touch-hole and fired. The shot was succeeded by the hiss of the cannon's priming, then the blaze and the crashing thunder of the monstrous gun burst upon the savages with such deafening roar that it seemed as if their very mountains had been rent asunder.

This was enough. The moment of surprise and hesitation caused by the unwonted sound gave us time to pass the point; a gentle breeze, which the dense foliage had hitherto prevented us from feeling, bulged out our sails; the schooner bent before it, and the shouts of the disappointed savages grew fainter and fainter in the distance as we were slowly wafted out to sea.

CHAPTER XXVI

During the greater part of that day I had been subjected to severe mental and much physical excitement, which had almost crushed me. But when the expedition whose failure has just been narrated was planned, my anxieties and energies had been so powerfully aroused that I went through the protracted scenes of that terrible night without a feeling of the slightest fatigue. No sooner was the last thrilling fear of danger past than my faculties were utterly relaxed; and when I felt the cool breezes of the Pacific playing around my fevered brow, and heard the free waves rippling at the schooner's prow, as we left the hated island behind us, my senses forsook me and I fell in a swoon upon the deck.

From this state I was quickly aroused by Bill, who shook me by the arm saying:

'Hallo, Ralph boy! rouse up, lad; we're safe now. Poor thing! I believe he's fainted.' And raising me in his arms he laid me on the folds of the gaff-top-sail, which lay upon the deck near the tiller. 'Here, take a drop o' this; it'll do you good, my boy,' he added, in a voice of tenderness which I had never heard him use before, while he held a brandy-flask to my lips.

I raised my eyes gratefully as I swallowed a mouthful; next moment my head sank heavily upon my arm, and I fell fast asleep. I slept long, for when I awoke the sun was a good way above the horizon. I did not move on first opening my eyes, as I felt a delightful sensation of rest pervading me. How long I would have lain in contemplation of this peaceful scene I do not know, but my mind was recalled suddenly and painfully to the past and the present by the sight of Bill, who was seated on the deck at my feet with his head reclining, as if in sleep, on his right arm, which rested on the tiller. As he seemed to rest peacefully, I did not mean to disturb him, but the slight noise I made in raising myself on my elbow caused him to start and look round.

'Well, Ralph, awake at last, my boy; you have slept long and soundly,' he said, turning towards me.

On beholding his countenance I sprang up in anxiety. He was deadly pale, and his hair, which hung in dishevelled locks over his face, was clotted with blood. Blood also stained his hollow cheeks and covered the front of his shirt, which, with the greater part of his dress, was torn and soiled with mud.

'O Bill!' said I, with deep anxiety, 'what is the matter with you? You are ill. You must have been wounded.'

'Even so, lad, said Bill, in a deep soft voice, while he extended his huge frame on the couch from which I had just risen. 'I've got an ugly wound, I fear; and I've been waiting for you to waken, to ask you to get me a drop o' brandy and a mouthful o' bread from the cabin lockers. You seemed to sleep so sweetly, Ralph, that I didn't like to disturb you. But I don't feel up to much just now.'

I did not wait till he had done talking, but ran below immediately and returned in a few seconds with a bottle of brandy and some broken biscuit. He seemed much refreshed after eating a few morsels and drinking a long draught of water mingled with a little of the spirits. Immediately afterwards he fell asleep, and I watched him anxiously until he awoke, being desirous of knowing the nature and extent of his wound.

'Ha!' he exclaimed, on awaking suddenly, after a slumber of an hour, 'I'm the better of that nap, Ralph; I feel twice the man I was'; and he attempted to rise, but sank sack again immediately with a deep groan.

'Nay, Bill, you must not move, but lie still while I look at your wound. I'll make a comfortable bed for you here on deck, and get you some breakfast. After that you shall tell me how you got it. Cheer up, Bill,' I added, seeing that he turned his head away; 'you'll be all right in a little, and I'll be a capital nurse to you though I'm no doctor.'

I then left him, and lighted a fire in the caboose. While it was kindling, I went to the steward's pantry and procured the materials for a good breakfast, with which, in little more than half an hour, I returned to my companion. He seemed much better, and smiled kindly on me as I set before him a cup of coffee and a tray with several eggs and some bread on it.

'Now then, Bill,' said I cheerfully, sitting down beside him on the deck, 'let's fall to. I'm very hungry myself, I can tell you; but—I forgot—your wound,' I added, rising; 'let me look at it.'

I found that the wound was caused by a pistol-shot in the chest. It did not bleed much, and as it was on the right side, I was in hopes that it might not be very serious. But Bill shook his head. 'However,' said he, 'sit down, Ralph, and I'll tell you all about it.'

'You see, after we left the boat an' began to push through the bushes, we went straight for the line of my musket, as I had expected; but by some unlucky chance it didn't explode, for I saw the line torn away by the men's legs, and heard the click o' the lock; so I fancy the priming had got damp and didn't catch. I was in a great quandary now what to do, for I couldn't concoct in my mind, in the hurry, any good reason for firin' off my piece. But they say necessity's the mother of invention; so just as I was givin' it up and clinchin' my teeth to bide the worst o't and take what should come, a sudden thought came into my head. I stepped out before the rest, seemin' to be awful anxious to be at the savages, tripped my foot on a fallen tree, plunged head foremost into a bush, an', ov coorse, my carbine exploded! Then came such a screechin' from the camp as I never heard in all my life. I rose at once, and was rushing on with the rest, when the captain called a halt.

' "You did that a-purpose, you villain!" he said, with a tremendous oath, and drawin' a pistol from his belt, let fly right into my breast. I fell at once, and remembered no more till I was startled and brought round by the most awful yell I ever heard in my life. Jumpin' up, I looked round, and through the trees saw a fire gleamin' not far off, the light o' which showed me the captain and men tied hand and foot, each to a post, and the savages dancin' round them like demons. I had scarce looked for a second, when I saw one o' them go up to the captain flourishing a knife, and before I could wink he plunged it into his breast, while another yell, like the one that roused me, rang upon my ear. I didn't wait for more, but bounding up, went crashing through the bushes into the woods. The black fellows caught sight of me, however, but not in time to prevent me jumpin' into the boat, as you know.'

'But now, Bill,' said I, 'it behoves us to think about the future, and what course of action we shall pursue. Moreover, here comes a breeze, so we must make up our minds which way to steer.'

'Ralph, boy,' said my companion, 'it matters not to me which way we go. I fear that my time is short now. Go where you will; I'm content.'

'Well then, Bill, I think we had better steer to the Coral Island, and see what has become of my dear old comrades, Jack and Peterkin. I believe the island has no name, but the captain once pointed it out to me on the chart, and I marked it afterwards; so, as we know pretty well our position just now, I think I can steer to it. Then, as to working the vessel, it is true I cannot hoist the sails single-handed, but luckily we have enough of sail set already; and if it should come on to blow a squall, I could at least drop the peaks of the main and fore sails, and clew them up partially without help, and throw her head close into the wind, so as to keep her all shaking till the violence of the squall is past. And if we have continued light breezes, I'll rig up a complication of blocks and fix them to the top-sail halyards, so that I shall be able to hoist the sails without help. 'Tis true I'll require half a day to hoist them, but we don't need to mind that. Then I'll make a sort of erection on deck to screen you from the sun, Bill; and if you can only manage to sit beside the tiller and steer for two hours every day, so as to let me get a nap, I'll engage to let you off duty all the rest of the twenty-four hours. And if you don't feel able for steering, I'll lash the helm and heave-to, while I get you your breakfasts and dinners; and so we'll manage famously.'

Bill smiled faintly as I ran on this strain.

'And what will you do,' said he, 'if it comes on to blow?'

This question silenced me, while I considered what I should do in such a case. At length I laid my hand on his arm, and said, 'Bill, when a man has done all that he *can* do, he ought to leave the rest to God.'

After a short pause, Bill raised his eyes and said, 'Ralph, I've led a terrible life. I've gone from bad to worse. I've been a pirate three years now. It is true I did not choose the trade, but I was inveigled aboard this schooner, and kept here by force till I became reckless and at last joined them. Since that time my hand has been steeped in human blood again and again.'

The energy with which he said this, and the action with which it was accompanied, were too much for Bill. He sank back with a deep groan. As if the very elements sympathized with him, a low moan came sweeping over the sea.

'Hist, Ralph!' said Bill, opening his eyes; 'there's a squall coming, lad. Look alive, boy! Clew up the fore-sail. Drop the main-sail peak. Them squalls come quick sometimes.'

I had already started to my feet, and saw that a heavy squall was indeed bearing down on us. I instantly did as Bill desired, for the schooner was still lying motionless on the glassy sea. I observed with some satisfaction that the squall was bearing down on the larboard bow, so that it would strike the vessel in the position in which she would be best able to stand the shock. Having done my best to shorten sail, I returned aft, and took my stand at the helm.

'Now, boy,' said Bill, in a faint voice, 'keep her close to the wind.'

Almost before the words had left his lips the wind burst upon us, and the spray dashed over our decks. For a time the schooner stood it bravely, and sprang forward against the rising sea like a war-horse. Meanwhile clouds darkened the sky, and the sea began to rise in huge billows. There was still too much sail on the schooner, and as the gale increased, I feared that the masts would be torn out of her or carried away, while the wind whistled and shrieked through the strained rigging. Suddenly the wind shifted a point, a heavy sea struck us on the bow, and the schooner was almost laid on her beam-ends, so that I could scarcely keep my legs. At the same moment Bill lost his hold of the belaying-pin which had served to steady him, and he slid with stunning violence against the skylight. As he lay on the deck close beside me, I could see that the shock had rendered him insensible, but I did not dare to quit the tiller for an instant, as it required all my faculties, bodily and mental, to manage the schooner. For an hour the blast drove us along, while, owing to the sharpness of the vessel's bow and the press of canvas, she dashed through the waves instead of breasting over them, thereby drenching the decks with water fore and aft. At the end of that time the squall passed away, and left us rocking on the bosom of the agitated sea.

My first care, the instant I could quit the helm, was to raise Bill from the deck and place him on the couch. I then ran below for the brandy-bottle and rubbed his face and hands with it, and endeavoured to pour a little down his throat. But my efforts, although I continued them long and assiduously, were of no avail; as I let go the hand which I had been chafing, it fell heavily on the deck. I laid my hand over his heart, and sat for some time quite motionless; but there was no flutter there—the pirate was dead!

CHAPTER XXVII

It was with feelings of awe, not unmingled with fear, that I now seated myself on the cabin skylight and gazed upon the rigid features of my late comrade, while my mind wandered over his past history and contemplated with anxiety my present position. Alone, in the midst of the wide Pacific, having a most imperfect knowledge of navigation, and in a schooner requiring at least eight men as her proper crew! But I will not tax the reader's patience with a minute detail of my feelings and doings during the first few days that followed the death of my companion. I will merely mention that I tied a cannon-ball to his feet, and with feelings of the deepest sorrow consigned him to the deep.

For fully a week after that a steady breeze blew from the east, and as my course lay west and by north, I made rapid progress towards my destination. I could not take an observation, which I very much regretted, as the captain's quadrant was in the cabin; but from the day of setting sail from the island of the savages I had kept a dead reckoning, and as I knew pretty well now how much leeway the schooner made, I hoped to hit the Coral Island without much difficulty. In this I was the more confident that I knew its position on the chart (which I understood was a very good one), and so had its correct bearings by compass.

As the weather seemed now quite settled and fine, and as I had got into the trade-winds, I set about preparations for hoisting the top-sails. This was a most arduous task, and my first attempts were complete failures, owing, in a great degree, to my ignorance of mechanical forces. The first error I made was in applying my apparatus of blocks and pulleys to a rope which was too weak, so that the very first heave I made broke it in two. Afterwards, however, I came to proportion things more correctly.

After the tackling was prepared and in good working order, it took me the greater part of a day to hoist the main top-sail. As I could not steer and work at this at the same time, I lashed the helm in such a position that, with a little watching now and then, it kept the schooner on her proper course. By this means I was enabled also to go about the deck and down below for things that I wanted, as occasion required; also to cook and eat my victuals. But I did not dare to trust to this plan during the three hours of rest that I allowed myself at night, as the wind might have shifted, in which case I should have been blown far out of my course ere I awoke. I was, therefore, in the habit of heaving to during those three hours—that is, fixing the rudder and the sails in such a position as that by acting against each other they would keep the ship stationary.

Of course I was anxious lest another squall should come, but I made the best provision I could in the circumstances, and concluded that by letting go the weather-braces of the top-sails and the top-sail halyards at the same time, I should render these sails almost powerless. Besides this, I proposed to myself to keep a sharp look-out on the barometer in the cabin, and if I observed at any time a sudden fall in it, I resolved that I would instantly set about my multiform appliances for reducing sail, so as to avoid being taken unawares. Thus I sailed prosperously for two weeks, with a fair wind.

The only book I found on board, after a careful search, was a volume of Captain Cook's voyages. This, I suppose, the pirate captain had brought with him in order to guide him, and to furnish him with information regarding the islands of these seas. I found this a most delightful book indeed, and I not only obtained much interesting knowledge about the sea in which I was sailing, but I had many of my own opinions, derived from experience, corroborated, and not a few of them corrected.

On the evening of my fourteenth day I was awakened out of a nap into which I had fallen by a loud cry, and starting up I gazed around me. I was surprised and delighted to see a large albatross soaring majestically over the ship. I immediately took it into my head that this was the albatross I had seen at Penguin Island. I had, of course, no good reason for supposing this, but the idea occurred to me, I know not why, and I cherished it, and regarded the bird with as much affection as if he had been an old friend. He kept me company all that day, and left me as night fell.

Next morning, as I stood motionless and with heavy eyes at the helm—for I had not slept well—I began to weary anxiously for daylight, and peered towards the horizon, where I thought I observed something like a black cloud against the dark sky. Being always on the alert for squalls, I ran to the bow. There could be no doubt it was a squall, and as I listened I thought I heard the murmur of the coming gale. Instantly I began to work might and main at my cumbrous tackle for shortening sail, and in the course of an hour and a half had the most of it reduced—the top-sail yards down on the caps, the top-sails clewed up, the sheets hauled in, the main and fore peaks lowered, and the flying-jib down. While thus engaged the dawn advanced, and I cast an occasional furtive glance ahead in the midst of my labour. But now that things were prepared for the worst, I ran forward again and looked anxiously over the bow. I now heard the roar of the waves distinctly, and as a single ray of the rising sun gleamed over the ocean I saw—what? Could it be that I was dreaming?—that magnificent breaker with its ceaseless roar!—that mountain-top!—yes, once more I beheld the Coral Island!

CHAPTER XXVIII

I almost fell upon the deck with the tumult of mingled emotions that filled my heart as I gazed ardently towards my beautiful island. It was still many miles away, but sufficiently near to enable me to trace distinctly the well-remembered outlines of the two mountains. I went below for the telescope, and spent nearly ten minutes of the utmost impatience in vainly trying to get a focus, and in rubbing the skin nearly off my eyes, before I discovered that having taken off the large glass to examine the phosphoric water I had omitted to put it on again.

After that I looked up impatiently at the sails, which I now regretted having lowered so hastily, and for a moment thought of hoisting the main top-sail again; but recollecting that it would take me full half a day to accomplish, and that, at the present rate of sailing, two hours would bring me to the island, I immediately dismissed the idea.

The remainder of the time I spent in making feverish preparations for arriving and seeing my dear comrades. I remembered that they were not in the habit of rising before six, and as it was now only three, I hoped to arrive before they were awake. Moreover, I set about making ready to let go the anchor, resolving in my own mind that, as I knew the depth of water in the passage of the reef and within the lagoon, I would run the schooner in and bring up opposite the bower. Fortunately the anchor was hanging at the cathead, otherwise I should never have been able to use it. Now, I had only to cut the tackling, and it would drop of its own weight. After searching among the flags, I found the terrible black one, which I ran up to the peak. While I was doing this a thought struck me. I went to the powder-magazine, brought up a blank cartridge and loaded the big brass gun, which, it will be remembered, was unhoused when we set sail, and as I had no means of housing it, there it had stood, bristling alike at fair weather and foul all the voyage. I took care to grease its mouth well, and before leaving the fore part of the ship, thrust the poker into the fire.

All was now ready. A steady five-knot breeze was blowing, so that I was now not more than a quarter of a mile from the reef. I was soon at the entrance, and as the schooner glided quickly through, I glanced affectionately at the huge breaker, as if it had been the same one I had seen there when I bade adieu, as I feared for ever, to the island. On coming opposite the Water Garden, I put the helm hard down. The schooner came round with a rapid, graceful bend, and lost way just opposite the bower. Running forward, I let go the anchor, caught up the red-hot poker, applied it to the brass gun, and saluted the mountains with a *bang* such as had only once before broken their slumbering echoes!

Effective although it was, however, it was scarcely equal to the bang with which, instantly after, Peterkin bounded from the bower, in scanty costume, his eyeballs starting from his head with surprise and terror. One gaze he gave, one yell, and then fled into the bushes like a wild-cat. The next moment Jack went through exactly the same performance, the only difference being that his movements were less like those of Jack-in-the-box, though not less vigorous and rapid than those of Peterkin.

'Hallo!' I shouted, almost mad with joy, 'what ho! Peterkin! Jack! hallo! it's *me*!'

My shout was just in time to arrest them. They halted and turned round, and the instant I repeated the cry I saw that they recognized my voice, by both of them running at full speed towards the beach. I could no longer contain myself. Throwing off my jacket, I jumped overboard at the same moment that Jack bounded into the sea. In another moment we met in deep water, clasped each other round the neck, and sank, as a matter of course, to the bottom! We were wellnigh choked, and instantly struggled to the surface, where Peterkin was spluttering about like a wounded duck, laughing and crying by turns, and choking himself with salt water!

It would be impossible to convey to my reader, by description, an adequate conception of the scene that followed my landing on the beach, as we stood embracing each other indiscriminately in our dripping garments, and giving utterance to incoherent rhapsodies, mingled with wild shouts. It can be more easily imagined than described, so I will draw a curtain over this part of my history, and carry the reader forward over an interval of three days.

During the greater part of that period Peterkin did nothing but roast pigs, taro, and bread-fruit, and ply me with plantains, plums, potatoes, and cocoa-nuts, while I related to him and Jack the terrible and wonderful adventures I had gone through since we last met. After I had finished the account, they made me go all over it again; and when I had concluded the second recital, I had to go over it again, while they commented upon it piecemeal. After they had 'pumped me dry', as Peterkin said, I begged to be informed of what had happened to them during my long absence, and particularly as to how they got out of the Diamond Cave.

'Well, you must know,' began Jack, 'after you had dived out of the cave, on the day you were taken away from us, we waited very patiently for half an hour, not expecting you to return before the end of that time. Then we began to upbraid you for staying so long, when you knew we would be anxious; but when an hour passed, we became alarmed, and I resolved at all hazards to dive out, and see what had become of you, although I felt for poor Peterkin, because, as he truly said, "If you never come back I'm shut up here for life." However, I promised not to run any risk, and he let me go; which, to say truth, I thought very courageous of him!'

'I should just think it was,' interrupted Peterkin, looking at Jack over the edge of a monstrous potato which he happened to be devouring at the time.

'Well,' continued Jack, 'you may guess my consternation when you did not answer to my halloo. At first I imagined that the pirates must have killed you, and left you in the bush or thrown you into the sea; then it occurred to me that this would have served no end of theirs, so I came to the conclusion that they must have carried you away with them. As this thought struck me, I observed the pirate schooner standing away to the nor'ard, almost hull down on the horizon, and I sat down on the rocks to watch her as she slowly sank from my sight. And I tell you, Ralph, my boy, that I shed more tears that time at losing you than I have done, I verily believe, all my life before. Well, after the schooner had disappeared, I dived back into the cave, much to Peterkin's relief, and told him what I had seen. We sat down and had a long talk over this matter, and then we agreed to make a regular systematic search through the woods, so as to make sure at least that you had not been killed. But now we thought of the difficulty of getting out of the cave without your help. Peterkin became dreadfully nervous when he thought of this; and I must confess that I felt some alarm, for, of course, I could not hope alone to take him out so quickly as we two together had brought him in; and he himself vowed that, if we had been a moment longer with him that time, he would have had to take a breath of salt water. However, there was no help for it, and I endeavoured to calm his fears as well as I could: "for," said I, "you can't live here, Peterkin"; to which he replied, "Of course not, Jack; I can only die here, and as that's not at all desirable, you had better propose something." So I suggested that he should take a good long breath, and trust himself to me.

‘ "Might we not make a large bag of cocoa-nut cloth, into which I could shove my head, and tie it tight round my neck?" he asked, with a haggard smile. "It might let me get one breath under water!"

‘ "No use," said I; "it would fill in a moment and suffocate you. I see nothing for it, Peterkin, if you really can't keep your breath so long, but to let me knock you down, and carry you out while in a state of insensibility."

‘But Peterkin didn't relish this idea. He seemed to fear that I could not be able to measure the exact force of the blow, and might, on the one hand, hit him so softly as to render a second or third blow necessary, which would be very uncomfortable; or, on the other hand, give him such a smash as would entirely spoil his figure-head, or mayhap knock the life out of him altogether! At last I got him persuaded to try to hold his breath, and commit himself to me; so he agreed, and down we went. But I had not got him half-way through, when he began to struggle and kick like a wild bull, burst from my grasp, and hit against the roof of the tunnel. I was therefore obliged to, force him violently back into the cave again, where he rose panting to the surface. In short he had lost his presence of mind, and——"

'Nothing of the sort,' cried Pertekin indignantly, 'I had only lost my wind; and if I had not had presence of mind enough to kick as I did, I should have bu'st in your arms!'

'Well, well, so be it,' resumed Jack with a smile; 'but the upshot of it was, that we had to hold another consultation on the point, and I really believe that, had it not been for a happy thought of mine, we should have been consulting there yet.'

'I wish we had,' interrupted Peterkin with a sigh. 'I'm sure, Ralph, if I had thought that you were coming back again, I would willingly have awaited your return for months, rather than have endured the mental agony which I went through! But proceed.'

'The thought was this,' continued Jack, 'that I should tie Peterkin's hands and feet with cords, and then lash him firmly to a stout pole about five feet long, in order to render him quite powerless, and keep him straight and stiff. You should have seen his face of horror, Ralph, when I suggested this; but he came to see that it was his only chance, and told me to set about it as fast as I could; "for," said he, "this is no jokin', Jack, I can tell you, and the sooner it's done the better." I soon procured the cordage and a suitable pole, with which I returned to the cave, and lashed him as stiff and straight as an Egyptian mummy; and, to say truth, he was no bad representation of what an English mummy would be, if there were such things, for he was as white as a dead man.

' "Now," said Peterkin, in a tremulous voice, "swim with me as near to the edge of the hole as you can before you dive, then let me take a long breath, and as I shan't be able to speak after I've taken it, you'll watch my face, and the moment you see me wink—dive! And oh, pray don't be long!"

'I promised to pay the strictest attention to his wishes, and swam with him to the outlet of the cave. Here I paused. "Now then," said I, "pull away at the wind, lad."

'Peterkin drew in a breath so long that I could not help thinking of the frog in the fable, that wanted to swell itself as big as an ox. Then I looked into his face earnestly. Slap went the lid of his right eye; down went my head, and up went my heels. We shot through the passage like an arrow, and rose to the surface of the open sea before you could count twenty.

'Peterkin had taken in such an awful load of wind that, on reaching the free air, he let it out with a yell loud enough to have been heard a mile off, and then the change in his feelings was so sudden and great, that he did not wait till we landed, but began, tied up as he was, to shout and sing for joy as I supported him with my left arm to the shore. However, in the middle of a laugh that a hyena might have envied, I let him accidentally slip, which extinguished him in a moment.

'After this happy deliverance, we immediately began our search for your dead body, Ralph; and you have no idea how low our hearts sank as we set off, day after day, to examine the valleys and mountain sides with the utmost care. In about three weeks we completed the survey of the whole island, and had at least the satisfaction of knowing that you had not been killed. But it occurred to us that you might have been thrown into the sea, so we examined the sands and the lagoon carefully, and afterwards went all round the outer reef. One day, while we were upon the reef, Peterkin espied a small dark object lying among the rocks, which seemed to be quite different from the surrounding stones. We hastened towards the spot, and found it to be a small keg. On knocking out the head we discovered that it was gunpowder.'

'It was I who sent you that, Jack,' said I, with a smile.

'Fork out!' cried Peterkin energetically, starting to his feet and extending his open hand to Jack.

'I'll give you an I O U in the meantime,' returned Jack, laughing, 'so sit down and be quiet.—The fact is, Ralph, when we discovered this keg of powder, Peterkin immediately took me a bet of a thousand pounds that you had something to do with it, and I took him a bet of ten thousand that you had not.'

'Peterkin was right then,' said I, explaining how the thing had occurred.

'Well, we found it very useful,' continued Jack, 'although some of it had got a little damp; and we furbished up the old pistol, with which Peterkin is a crack shot now. But to continue: We did not find any other vestige of you on the reef, and finally gave up all hope of ever seeing you again. After this the island became a dreary place for us, and we began to long for a ship to heave in sight and take us off. But now that you're back again my dear fellow, it looks as bright and cheerful as it used to do.

'And now,' continued Jack, 'I have a great desire to visit some of the other islands of the South Seas. Here we have a first-rate schooner at our disposal, so I don't see what should hinder us.'

'Just the very thing I was going to propose,' cried Peterkin. 'I vote for starting at once.'

I need scarcely say that having made up our minds to go, we lost no time in making preparations to quit the island; and as the schooner was well laden with stores of every kind for a long cruise, we had little to do except to add to our abundant supply a quantity of cocoa-nuts, bread-fruit, taro, yams, plums, and potatoes, chiefly with the view of carrying the fragrance of our dear island along with us as long as we could.

When all was ready, we paid a farewell visit to the different familiar spots where most of our time had been spent. We ascended the mountain-top and gazed for the last time at the rich green foliage in the valleys, the white sandy beach, the placid lagoon, and the barrier coral reef with its crested breakers. Then we descended to Spouting Cliff, and looked down at the pale-green monster which we had made such fruitless efforts to spear in days gone by. From this we hurried to the Water Garden, and took a last dive into its clear waters, and a last gambol amongst its coral groves. I hurried out before my companions, and dressed in haste, in order to have a long examination of my tank, which Peterkin, in the fullness of his heart, had tended with the utmost care, as being a vivid remembrancer of me rather than out of love for natural history. It was in superb condition—the water as clear and pellucid as crystal; the red and green sea-weed of the most brilliant hues; the red, purple, yellow, green and striped anemones fully expanded, and stretching out their arms as if to welcome and embrace their former master; the star-fish, zoophytes, sea-pens and other innumerable marine insects looking fresh and beautiful; and the crabs, as Peterkin said, looking as wide awake, impertinent, rampant, and pugnacious as ever. It was indeed so lovely and so interesting that I would scarcely allow myself to be torn away from it.

Last of all, we returned to the bower and collected the few articles we possessed, such as the axe, the pencil-case, the broken telescope, the penknife, the hook made from the brass ring, and the sail-needle, with which we had landed on the island; also the long boots and the pistol, besides several curious articles of costume which we had manufactured from time to time.

These we conveyed on board in our little boat, after having carved our names on a chip of iron-wood, thus:—

JACK MARTIN,
RALPH ROVER,
PETERKIN GAY,

which we fixed up inside of the bower. The boat was then hoisted on board and the anchor weighed, which latter operation cost us great labour and much time, as the anchor was so heavy that we could not move it without the aid of my complex machinery of blocks and pulleys. A steady breeze was blowing off shore when we set sail, at a little before sunset. It swept us quickly past the reef and out to sea. The shore grew rapidly more indistinct as the shades of evening fell, while our clipper bark bounded lightly over the waves. Slowly the mountain-top sank on the horizon, until it became a mere speck. In another moment the sun and the Coral Island sank together into the broad bosom of the Pacific.

Our voyage during the next two weeks was most interesting and prosperous. The breeze continued generally fair, and at all times enabled us to lie our course; for being, as I have said before, clipper-built, the pirate schooner could lie very close to the wind and make little leeway. We had no difficulty now in managing our sails, for Jack was heavy and powerful, while Peterkin was active as a kitten. Still, however, we were quite an insufficient crew for such a vessel. Although we could now manage our sails easily, we nevertheless found that my pulleys were of much service to us in some things; though Jack did laugh heartily at the uncouth arrangement of ropes and blocks, which had, to a sailor's eye, a very lumbering and clumsy appearance. But I will not drag my reader through the details of this voyage. Suffice it to say that, after an agreeable sail of about three weeks, we arrived off the island of Mango, Tararo's island, which I recognized at once from the description that the pirate Bill had given me of it during one of our conversations.

There, three natives volunteered to go with us to Tahiti, where we thought it likely that we should be able to procure a sufficient crew of sailors to man our vessel; so we accepted their offer gladly.

It was a bright clear morning when we hoisted the snow-white sails of the pirate schooner and left the shores of Mango. Thousands of the natives came down to see us sail away. As the vessel bent before a light fair wind, we glided quickly over the lagoon under a cloud of canvas.

That night as we sat on the taffrail gazing out upon the wide sea and up into the starry firmament, a thrill of joy, strangely mixed with sadness, passed through our hearts; for we were at length 'homeward bound', and were gradually leaving far behind us the beautiful bright green coral islands of the Pacific Ocean.

OTHER TITLES IN THIS SERIES